Mouth

Mouth

stories

Puloma Ghosh

ASTRA HOUSE
NEW YORK

Various stories from this collection first appeared in the following collections:
"K" in *One Story*; "In the Winter" in *CRAFT*; and "Natalya" in *Cutleaf.*

Astra House
A Division of Astra Publishing House
astrahouse.com
Printed in the United States of America

Library of Congress Cataloging-in-Publication Data
Names: Ghosh, Puloma, author.
Title: Mouth : stories / Puloma Ghosh.
Description: First edition. | New York : Astra House, 2024. | Summary: "Mouth is
an eerie, uncanny debut collection of speculative stories that moves across time
and place, blurring the lines of conventional reality"—Provided by publisher.
Identifiers: LCCN 2023051011 (print) | LCCN 2023051012 (ebook) |
ISBN 9781662602474 (hardcover) | ISBN 9781662602467 (epub)
Subjects: LCGFT: Short stories.
Classification: LCC PS3607.H668 M68 2024 (print) | LCC PS3607.H668 (ebook) |
DDC 813/.6—dc23/eng/20231127
LC record available at https://lccn.loc.gov/2023051011
LC ebook record available at https://lccn.loc.gov/2023051012

First edition
10 9 8 7 6 5 4 3 2 1

Design by Alissa Theodor
The text is set in Warnock Pro.
The titles are set in GT Sectra Display.

For my mother and grandmothers
and the scary stories they told me at night

Contents

Mouth

Desiccation

Ma wanted me to befriend the only other Indian girl at our skating rink because Ma knew the rest of the girls didn't like me. She imagined Pritha and I would be fast friends just because we looked more like each other than we did everyone else. I now think Ma only wanted another mother to commiserate with, one who didn't ignore her while she sat in the stands during competitions, wearing her ridiculous puffy coat. Someone from her own country might have been more sympathetic to the choices Ma made, less fearful of the person she'd become. My mother had been alone for a long time, ever since they took my father with all the men years ago. I'm sure she had friends once, but I hardly remember a time before she took the job at the Bureau and everyone in town stopped speaking to her. At that age, I thought my aloneness was a choice, a badge of individuality, but my mother knew it was a consequence of her own choices, and that's probably why it bothered her to see me stretch alone.

The night before the winter competition, Ma and I made our weekly trip to the shop. She handed me a can and said, "Just talk to her, Meghna. You'll find that you have a lot in common."

I didn't know how to explain to her that Pritha didn't strike me as descended from any nationality. The only adult I'd ever seen her with was her coach. Pritha had a singularity that felt like it couldn't have an origin. I was fairly certain she wasn't even human.

To avoid answering, I rearranged the items in our cart—cans at the bottom, boxes up top.

"She wants to talk to you, I can tell," Ma insisted. "She's always watching you."

I didn't find this comforting.

Pritha was pale, slim, and lithe. Everything about her had precision but no warmth. She rocked smoothly from the inside of her blade to the outside, her body a sail against the wind. She was terrifying when she competed, waxy cheeks split by an uncanny lipsticked smile. She always won gold, as though the judges were afraid to give her anything less, and I was always stuck a step below with silver.

Pritha never smiled on the podium. In all the pictures that lined the rink's office during the past three years that she'd lived here, she stood expressionless. I think we must have been the same age, but beside her, with my toothy, white grin, I looked like a child.

I expected the winter competition to be like all the others, with me and her taking first and second. There were only a handful of girls in town who competed year after year, and of them, we were the best. Tiny and aerodynamic, equally hardworking, she and I had the most ice time booked each week and flew through our jumps like gravity was nothing. By the time I got to high school, the other girls were more concerned about competing with one another and ignored us for the most part.

But midroutine that day, I couldn't help but remember my mother's words. I thought of Pritha's gaze for only a split second, a crucial mistake, as I twisted over my left shoulder to prepare for a double Axel, the most difficult element in my program. I shifted my weight to my left foot, swinging my right and using that motion to launch into the air. I closed my eyes, and the rink went black. Cold air cupped my cheeks, my molars pressed neatly together in the back of my mouth. My body, which had been clenched tight, unwound after my second rotation, knowing from hours of practice where and when to spring open, and catch the ice back on my blade. On landing, I saw Pritha there, her face stark white like a summoned ghost against the shadowed risers, clear as if she were standing on the ice with me. The music continued, but I couldn't move, numbed by her fixed look. My ankle gave out, and I slid across the rink, at the mercy of my own momentum. The cold chafe of rough ice on my bare arms jolted sensation back into my body. When I looked up, my coach was hurrying across the ice toward me, and Pritha was gone, buried once more in the crowd.

I had seen corpses, which is why I knew Pritha was not alive. Baba did autopsies before the Bureau relocated him to who-knows-where when I was seven. In middle school, I started snooping around his things. After Ma went to sleep, I often snuck into his old study and opened drawers, peeking into folders of coroner's reports. One day I turned on his computer. His passwords were easy—my birthday or Ma's. I scrolled through the photographs he left behind: women and men naked on steel tables, sutures across their chests. Crime scenes dotted with yellow tabs, and a body gleaming under the flash like fresh ice.

Pritha looked like she had climbed out of one of those photographs and pulled on a skating dress. Her face was blank; her flesh appeared hard and painted. In a locker room full of teenage girls, she was a plastic ball hidden poorly in a bowl of ripe plums. When she walked past, a morgue-like chill raised goose bumps on my skin.

I've always loved cold things—the hum of Popsicles against my teeth, the chlorine sting of pool water. Whenever my parents took me skating as a child, I would lie face down on the ice in a tantrum at the end of public skating, partially because I didn't want to leave and partially because I liked the way the cold against my cheek turned into pain and then nothing.

Ma said it was Baba's idea to start me with a coach, but I think this was a lie to make me love someone I barely remembered. Sometimes it felt like I missed him, but I was never sure if what I missed was really him or a father fabricated from the ones I'd seen on TV. And maybe it was because he was so unreal to me, so absent from even the places in the house that were once his, that I could find my darkest appetite in that study.

I touched myself for the first time there, photographs wallpapering the monitor. The softness of flesh against metal made me want to tense every muscle I had. Eyes open, lips parted, the bodies looked enraptured. They convinced me that death was akin to ecstasy, and imitating their contorted poses on the high-backed chair, I came.

Ma drove me to the clinic after the fall, my ankle wrapped in ice. On the way, we passed our house, then our neighbor Gabriel's. I noticed his driveway was still empty.

I turned to my mother's tired profile. For many years, she'd been enforcing the draft in our county. Our town called her the Collector, as though she were the one who kept the men shut away somewhere. Each time a boy turned seventeen, she had to escort him to the Bureau. After that, we never saw him again. If he tried to dodge, she'd disappear for hours, sometimes days, in pursuit. She always found him.

"Did you turn in Gabriel?" I asked her, even though it was a morbid question that would only make both of us feel bad. My raised foot, signaling weeks of skate-free boredom, had put me in a shitty mood.

"No," she replied, her eyes on the road.

"Where is he?"

"I don't know yet."

Yet. No wonder Ma was in a shitty mood too.

"They don't have to take everyone, do they? What happens if you let him go?"

She sighed. "Nothing good."

"Are you going to leave soon to look for him?"

Ma didn't answer, and I was afraid to ask again. I liked Gabriel. We had been neighbors for as long as I could remember, and he was the only friend I had at the rink. He drove me to practice sometimes, when Ma was gone. He had dark curls that writhed with their own life when he skated. Whenever he jumped, his clenched teeth left neat dimples by the sharp part of his jaw. He was the closest thing I'd seen to a man since I was a child.

One morning, a month before the winter competition, we sat in his truck, waiting for the coaches to come unlock the doors. It was still dark out. I had seen him become more sullen over the past few months because he no longer had anyone to compete against. Just shy of seventeen, he was the last remaining boy at our rink, and it was almost his time.

I touched his jaw, and he turned to me. "You're so lucky, Meg. You can be anything. You can skate forever."

I shook my head. "There is no forever. Nobody knows what the Bureau has planned."

He turned off his headlights and kissed me. We grasped for each other between the seats, and I bruised my pelvis on the stick shift. I shoved my hand into his pants and he turned hard, so jarringly warm in the cool dawn. He came quick and sticky in my palm. As we searched for napkins, I saw Pritha standing at the door to the rink. I don't know how long she had been watching, but her white face made me shiver. Gabriel wiped my hand gently, not noticing

8

her. I kept my eyes on Pritha until her coach arrived, and when I stepped out of the car, I was so wet my knees quivered.

Two weeks later, Gabriel stopped coming to the rink.

This is what we were told in school: There's a war going on, unlike any that preceded it. Eight years ago, things became so dire, they conscripted all the men in the country for a top-secret purpose. There were no battles we could see, no bloodshed on soil. Nobody could be trusted to know what was going on because we were surrounded by leaky technology that could see, hear, touch, read. Shortly after, they switched all communications to local: mobile devices bricked, internet access restricted to nearby servers, all packages and shipments thoroughly regulated, landlines hitting an apologetic operator when people tried to dial outside of their area codes.

Our world shrank, but after the initial shock and a few transitional years, most people in our town became comfortable. If there was unrest anywhere, we couldn't see it. Some even argued things became better for women, as the world was seldom good to them before, but that might have been propaganda fed to us by the Bureau. Even as a child, I wondered what was "good" about being left behind. We entertained ourselves with hobbies, competitions, books, and old movies. I was lucky that my town had a well-established skating rink before things fell apart. I twirled and twirled around the rink every day until I ached too much to think, but to say I could "be anything" was a stretch.

I tried to ask Ma many times where they took the men, but she always said she didn't know. I only came to believe her when I missed school after the injury. Lying on the couch during one of those days, I heard Ma in the kitchen. Her voice carried through the heating ducts and hissed perfectly out the radiator. "He's only a boy!" she whispered, and I knew she meant Gabriel. "What will you do with him?"

I was surprised to hear her ask this question outright. She never showed mercy or resistance; that was why everyone hated her so much. When parents cried and begged, she didn't flinch. But I thought of my mother smoothing bandages over Gabriel's elbows when we got little scrapes on the rink, when she gave him piano lessons in our living room. I felt so sad for her all of a sudden.

I could tell from the silence that she didn't get an answer. The Bureau never gave answers. The phone hit the table with a clatter, and her breathing became shallow. I turned on the television so I wouldn't have to hear her cry. I thought about Pritha instead. My gut told me if I hadn't met her eyes, I would have landed that jump like any other.

I still went to the rink for conditioning while I healed. For days I talked to no one but my coach, and it felt awful when I couldn't skate to keep busy. I came to terms with the fact that Gabriel was not coming back, leaving me friendless.

I was alone in the locker room feeling sorry for myself one day, when Pritha came in and sat down. She shuffled around in her bag for her lace puller and untied one skate. While she tightened it, I asked, "Was it you?"

She looked up.

"Did you make me fall?"

"It's beautiful." She tilted her head. "The way you fall."

"That's not how the judges felt."

"When you touch the ice, you come alive. Like you want it to hold you."

I had no idea what to say to that. The squeak of laces against leather echoed between us.

"Where are you from?" I asked at last, in an attempt to appease my mother's hopes.

She smiled. "Far away."

While I sat in silence, perplexed by her vague answer, she tied a knot, dropped the puller back into her bag, and left the locker room. I felt oddly relieved. I loved how little I knew about Pritha, how strangely she spoke. She didn't go to my school, and I didn't know where she lived. At the rink, we assumed she was homeschooled, but we were all too afraid of her to ask. She was just teeth and flesh and empty eyes, no different from a body on a slab.

In February, a rat infestation emerged in the neighborhood. We were told to keep our snacks in airtight containers—no bags or chewable wrappers or loose fruit in the locker room. The custodian stuck her broom into every corner of the rink, searching for vermin, but found nothing. A few days later, she discovered a pile of half-chewed rat corpses by the rink's dumpster.

"We must have cats," she told the concerned mothers.

One morning, as I paced around the rink with no Gabriel to kiss before the doors unlocked, I found Pritha crouched against the building's gray wall, her teeth deep in a crumpled rodent. I turned the corner before she saw me.

A few weeks later, the rat problem was under control, and I realized I hadn't seen a single cat outdoors, stray or collared, for many months.

Not long after, Pritha and I were alone in the locker room as we changed after practice. She finished early, having landed every jump perfectly, and I was still easing back into my regular routine. I noticed a scar between her neck and shoulder: pink and round, like teeth. I asked her what it was from.

"A tiger bit me long ago."

"Tigers are extinct," I said.

"They are now," she replied.

I stood up and walked toward her as she pulled a sweatshirt from her locker.

"Like this?" I sank my teeth into her scar, pressing them into the discolored skin.

She sighed and rolled her head back. "Yes. Yes, just like that."

I bit and sucked and ran my tongue along the hard, salty muscle. I pulled away with a wet sound. She exhaled and put her sweatshirt on. She left without another word, but I wished she had stayed and touched me. I loved how cold she was against my mouth.

"I think Pritha and I are friends now," I told Ma.

"Good." She smiled and plucked a can of spinach from the kitchen cabinet. "Where are her parents from?"

"I don't think she has any."

Ma set the can on the counter and shuffled through a drawer. I heard the scrape of a can opener slicing through metal. She didn't seem surprised, but I could tell she was sad. I didn't know how long it had been since she had spoken to someone from her home country. Probably not since Baba left. If there were more of us in the area, I hadn't met them.

People hadn't always been afraid of Ma. She used to be a music teacher who went to barbecues and PTA meetings. I only remember this version of her from photos and fuzzy memories of long hair and floral patterns, her neck smelling like perfume. The preschool she had worked at closed a few years after the men were taken. The children grew older, but not enough new ones were born. The price of sperm kept going up, and everyone was hesitant: What if the baby was a boy?

I think it was my fault that she became the Collector. I remember for some time, while she taught private voice and piano lessons, she took me out of skating practice. I threw tantrums—silent one moment, screaming another, always uncooperative. I refused to do chores or homework in protest. Then one day she stopped singing and started disappearing, and then the next month I had a coach, a pair of leather skates, and a closet full of little velvet dresses. By the time I was old enough to realize what had happened, it felt too late to change course. Or maybe I just told myself this because I didn't want to stop skating.

Ma still loved music. At night she played classical songs so loudly, the sitar and tabla and crescendo of vocals carried through our whole cul-de-sac. The neighbors complained, but she didn't care. Even if there were no lights, no moon, no stars, you could have found our house from its sound.

One afternoon, Pritha caught me leaving the locker room and said, "Come with me." It was the first time she approached me herself. My curfew wasn't for some time, so I followed her out the back door. I remembered the mangled rats. We were so used to people disappearing. Taken or killed, it made no difference if they never returned. If I disappeared too, would anyone have bothered to search for me? Ma always told me we had to accept the logic of the world we were given and learn to live in it. Maybe she would have let that logic swallow me like it swallowed my father, his warm hands, the buttons on his cuffs that were once larger than my fingernails.

We crossed the street to the shop. It was vacant at that hour, with only two cashiers calling SKU numbers and then item names at each other in some kind of game. We walked through the aisles silently until I asked, "Did you want to get something?"

"No. I just like how it smells in here."

All shops smelled the same: like the crisp nothing of packaged food.

"Are they different where you're from?"

"I don't know. I haven't been back in a long time. Most shops are probably like this one by now." She touched a box. "When I was young, they smelled like sweat in the summer, like earth and fruit. Like raw meat, fresh fish. It was sweet and putrid at once."

"That sounds kind of gross."

"It was. But the boxes and bottles were all different colors. Every aisle a rainbow. Can you imagine it?"

I couldn't, but I wanted to. I stood close to her in the empty aisle. She didn't move away when I pressed my cheek against hers, rubbing my nose into her ear. She smelled different from anyone I'd known. Like raw meat, fresh fish. I grasped her hand and moved it under my skirt. "Tell me more."

She slid her fingers under my leotard and whispered of dust and humid air, crowded streets teeming with screens and overlapping voices. I knew without a doubt she wasn't human but something born in a version of the world I'd never witnessed. Rather than afraid, I was incredibly aroused. I wanted her to take me far away from that featureless white aisle, someplace beyond the handful of streets that had been—and I thought always would be—all I knew. I rocked against her fingertips and learned that pleasure is another form of taking. It wrings you of moisture until you're parched and trembling against the dry goods. She brought me to my knees and then stuck both her fingers into her mouth, sucking hard before wiping them on her sweatshirt and leaving.

At dinner, Ma stared at me for a long time, like she knew I was different. She wanted to tell me something. I closed my legs under the table and tried not to look at her.

I didn't need the computer or photos that night. I only imagined Pritha lying on the tiled floor of the shop, her arms and legs spread askew, numbered yellow tags leading me to her body and flat black eyes.

I woke up the next morning with blood stuck between my thighs. As I made my way to my mom's bathroom to see if she had any extra pads, I found her bed empty and cold, like it had never been slept in.

I wanted Pritha to suck me dry. She was an anomaly—the Bureau made all the rules but didn't seem to know or care about her. I preferred her teeth to whatever the world had planned for me. At least she would leave a body if she killed me, and everyone would know that I was really, truly gone. I remembered the way she held the rat. She was careful, even tender, as though it was a broken trinket she wanted to mend. It was a personal act.

The night before my first program since the injury, Ma still hadn't returned home. It had been nearly a week, which was unusual even for her, and soon I would run out of food. At two A.M., I accepted that I would have to prep for the show on my own. I folded my tights and costume and tucked them into my backpack with our makeup pouch. I made sure they were all there—the velvet scrunchie, the bobby pins—and left early so I wouldn't have to stay in that dark house alone.

It took half an hour to walk to the rink. Pritha was already in the parking lot when I arrived. She looked the same as she would have any other day: leaning against the fence, wearing a hoodie over her costume.

"Do you live here?" I asked her.

"I don't live anywhere," she replied.

"How did you know I'd be here early?"

"I didn't." She flashed her teeth when she said that to me, but in the dark, I couldn't tell if any of them were pointed. This was as close to a laugh as I had ever seen her manage.

Pritha had her coach's keys. We went into the rink and turned all the lights on. We walked out onto the ice and stripped naked. She let me crawl on top of her and lick her, bite her. Her skin wouldn't break, and there was no blood; my teeth left white imprints like I was biting into chewed gum. She sucked the blood between my legs over and over until I twisted and cried out. She was so eager; it almost hurt as much as it felt good. Her eyes gleamed brighter each time she came back to smother me with a metallic kiss. Every inch of her was so cold, I began to shiver. My tongue turned numb.

"Did you make me sprain my ankle?" I asked with my fingers plunged in icy wetness, her eyes shut tight. She whimpered, and I asked again.

"Yes," she admitted at last. "Yes, yes. I wanted to see the ice touch you. I wanted you to touch the ice while thinking of me."

I begged her to bite me, but she wouldn't. She never even let me see all her teeth. The ice left little red scuffs on my shoulder blades, elbows, anything that protruded, and she put her mouth on each wound. Our voices echoed in the monstrous rink. I wanted to die there. When detectives found us, they would mark our tangled limbs with bright tags, take high-flash photographs of my curled toes.

"I did something I shouldn't have last night," Pritha said in the locker room after we dressed. "I have to leave now." It was almost daylight. Soon the rink would flood with skaters and coaches and parents.

"Will you tell me something before you go?" I asked, trying to pretend I wasn't expecting a beginning rather than an end.

"Anything."

"Are you a vampire?"

"What is that?" She blinked, and I almost lost my nerve.

"Don't pretend. What else could you be?"

She smiled, her lips turning white as they stretched. "A girl, the same as you."

Pritha stood and took her skates from her locker. She placed them in her bag one at a time. I grasped her sleeve. "Take me with you."

"Where?"

"Anywhere."

With no blood, Pritha had no current pulling her—only the wind through her hollow veins. She skated so well because every movement was her own. Maybe if she drained me, it wouldn't matter that my life was already drained of everyone I loved.

She gently pulled out of my grip. "You don't want that."

"Please, don't leave me. I don't think my mother is coming home." I sounded like a child. I was a child.

"There's nothing I can do about that, Meghna." She said my name like only my mother could, with that soft *gh*. She touched my cheek. There was some girl in her but very little. The rest was something I didn't understand, that I would never understand. "Do you spin with your eyes open or shut?" she asked.

I looked at my hands. I didn't want to cry in front of her. "I'm not sure. I've never thought about it."

"I keep mine open."

I pictured Pritha's layback, its perfect arch, her arms reaching up toward the rafters.

"What do you see?" I asked.

"Everything."

Her cold touch left my skin. I heard her walk out, but I didn't look up to watch her leave. Instead I laced my skates.

When my turn to perform came, I glided to the center of the rink. With Pritha gone, I was sure to be the best skater at the rink, a gold medalist. I landed every jump with full rotations and balanced check-outs. My step sequence was a clean blend of staccato and buttery twizzles; my flying camel touched down at a perfect right angle. When I wound up for my layback, I thought of Pritha and opened my eyes wide. The ceiling was a gray-white blur, like a blank sheet of paper. Violins crescendoed, and I began to wobble. I wasn't like Pritha. I was full of blood that pumped fear and loneliness and longing in and out of me until I became dizzy. I stumbled through the last notes of my program. Hours later, I walked home alone with another silver medal. Night fell, and I realized everything had changed.

The next day they found Pritha's coach drained of blood, curled up like a sleeping cat in the parking lot of the shop. Within that next week, we all realized that the Bureau sent my mother away for insubordination—she couldn't, wouldn't turn in Gabriel—and the town loved her more once she was missing than they had when she was there.

Many years later, a sharply dressed woman from the Bureau came to my door to offer me my mother's job. As I made her tea in my little kitchenette, I thought of Pritha, the way she slalomed over the ice like a clean sheet of paper drifting off a desk by someone's elbow. A strange thing unnoticed until it disappeared. Though she refused to take me or my blood, knowing her had sucked something out of me, and over time, its absence left deeper and deeper cracks. I accepted the offer and drove beyond the town limits for the first time since I was a child. I would go looking for Ma, because fuck this world's logic. I can be an anomaly too. I never saw Pritha again, but I still remember that spinning ceiling, how everything and nothing looked the same.

The Fig Tree

The summer after her marriage, Ankita returns with her father to the city where she was born, her mother's ashes tucked under her arm in a thermos-like silver jar. Calcutta had turned into Kolkata in Ankita's absence, with fresh blue-and-white paint along sidewalks and fences. In the years since she had last visited, the open pastures around the airport had grown shoots of half-built highrises, mazelike around the highway. It's now almost monsoon season. Recent rainfall marks the streets at every dip—glassy pools lit by the string lights that cling wild to every tree and pole.

"It's clean," Ankita says to her father as the taxi stops at a red light. The road looks desolate without bright spots of plastic and shards of terra-cotta. The driver, hearing English, waits for a green despite the lack of traffic.

"So it is," her father says in Bengali, a switch flipped easily. "Mamata's work."

The driver snorts. "Next time you come, it'll be dirty again. Not a single light will turn on."

Ankita would prefer to see more waste, more remnants of the city populating Kolkata in the hours when it is sparse of people. That would make her homecoming feel more like home. She's already unsettled to be in the wide leather seat of this taxi without her mother's hot arm pressed against hers. The emptiness out there makes the emptiness inside the car yawn wider. The years with no memories here feel like a place she can sink into and disappear, the way her mother had.

A woman emerges from an alley, a red spot against the shuttered stores. The back of her neck looks familiar, the same curve Ankita traced on her mother's spine in her earliest memories. Ankita feels like this woman was summoned from a very specific longing that has been teasing Ankita in the months since her mother's death, always just out of her reach. She presses her hand against the window. The woman stops and raises her head like a cat, as though she feels the light touch of Ankita's fingertips and palm. The woman begins to turn around, but the car lurches into motion, and Ankita never sees her face. She recedes as the car picks up speed, pushed from sight just as Ankita pushes the ever-threatening lump down her throat with a hard swallow.

Ankita's father has only one sibling—his sister, Sujata. She's dozing in an armchair when they arrive, her stomach held like a beach ball in her lap. Ankita kneels to touch her aunt's feet, and she wakes with a start, holds her niece's face, and says, "At last, you've come," as though she has been waiting a decade in that chair. It's been so long since Ankita last saw her face without pixels, she's shocked at how smooth and clean her aunt's skin looks despite its new creases. "You must be tired," Sujata says, and Ankita nods, suddenly heavy, and lays her head on that long-forgotten lap.

"I could have come," Ankita's husband, David, says over video chat the next morning. It's a strange twilit hour between the animal sounds of night and the human racket of day.

"It's too hot here," Ankita says, smiling and brushing stray hairs from her face. "Just look at my hair. You would die."

"It's fine." David looks tired even on video. "I wanted to come."

Ankita knew this all along but pretended not to when her father proposed the trip. She booked her single ticket without offering to take David along. "We'll come another time," she assures him. "On a better occasion, at a cooler time of year."

Truthfully, she can't imagine being here with anyone but her parents, sharing a wide bed in a relative's apartment. David is tall and light-haired, terrible at pronouncing even the simplest Bengali words. She would have no idea what to do with him. She's thankful the call ends quickly so he can get ready for bed. She doesn't want to stare any longer at the *why* he asks with his eyes, even when he can't say it out loud.

Jet lag makes daytime a yellowed dream. Ankita can only be awake for hours at a time, unsure whether she's in Sujata's small fourth-floor apartment or the buttercream-pastel rooms of her grandmother's old house. Pink, yellow, mint green. In Ankita's dreams, her mother's demanding voice rouses her from bed, just like in the Saturdays of her childhood. "Laziness runs in your father's family," Ankita's mother declares as she tugs away sheets and blankets. "I don't want to see you lying around all morning like your aunt."

Life is stagnant at Sujata's apartment. She's a widow who sits in the same chair for most of the day while Aparna, the woman who does her chores, fans herself in front of the television between tasks.

"Can we go to Amma's house?" Ankita asks between sips of tea on the second morning. She had always stayed at her grandmother's house when she was in Kolkata, but nobody has lived there since her grandmother's death.

"Why?" her aunt asks, wrinkling her nose. "That place is falling apart."

"I just want to see it."

Sujata shakes her head. "There's nothing there but ghosts."

"Ghosts are just memories," Ankita insists.

"No, they're not," Sujata says with such finality, Ankita is afraid to ask again.

Aparna turns off the fan to sweep, and Ankita dips into another doze. When the humid air grows still, it's impossible not to. Her grandmother's house tugs at her. She doesn't know if it's nostalgia or a way of missing her mother and even her grandmother. Ankita longs for familiar skin, the sheen of sweat behind their ears, hair glistening with sweet hibiscus oil. The heat-and-lotion smell she's grasped for all her life.

When was the last time Ankita held her mother? At her and David's wedding, maybe. It wasn't something she thought to do often as an adult, and now she wonders why. Her mother's body doesn't yet feel like something out of Ankita's reach. So far, her passing has felt like a long separation. It happened on a rare day in March that parted the clouds. Ankita's mother was in the sunlit kitchen while Ankita's father worked in the garden. Her mother's life was sliced quick as ripe fruit under a sharp knife: heart attack, DOA. She had already stopped breathing when Ankita's father found her. She died alone on the new tiles she picked at The Home Depot just before her daughter's wedding. If Ankita went into that kitchen now, she might expect her mother to still be there, dropping fritters into hot oil.

But now, Ankita is alone in Kolkata, a place she has never been without her mother. The house they always slept in sits abandoned in a different part of the city. The cousins who had once dropped by daily to keep her company currently work tech jobs in bigger cities with families of their own. Her grandparents' generation has mostly passed away. Without them, this city is a stranger to her. She is beginning to realize that she's never set foot in it alone, and more than that, she's afraid to. Early each morning, her father leaves with the rental car to explain his wife's death to what's left of their extended family. He never offers to take her along, and she doesn't feel like she can leave the apartment without him. What once felt like the warmest, fullest place she knew now gapes vast and hostile beyond barred windows.

Ankita wakes to clattering bangles. She expects to feel her mother's wrist on her cheek, smooth fingers against Ankita's ear. Instead she finds Aparna crouched at her feet, bangles shuddering as she drags the broom under Ankita's chair.

"I want marriage bangles," Ankita tells her aunt, who is leaning sideways, scrutinizing Aparna's work under the furniture.

Sujata straightens and says, "About time."

Sujata refuses to take Ankita out by auto or rickshaw, not when she's so unaccustomed to heat and pollution. They lie in front of the AC for hours, waiting for Ankita's father to return with the car. The city languishes in the long, bright day. Ankita wakes from another nap as her father spreads himself, freshly showered, on the bed beside her and says, "This is good. The sun won't be as hot by the time you leave," as if it mattered in the air-conditioned car.

Sujata is already up and telling him about their outing. Ankita drags herself slowly from the deathlike sleep of a foreign time zone. She tiptoes into the kitchen for a slice of bread—a small independence after days of Aparna beating her to every task. The day wanes across the combined living-dining room. On one wall, the doors to the balcony are flung wide open to let in whatever breeze the day can muster. Dusk has peached everything.

A sliver of Aparna's back peeks out between swaths of fabric hanging to dry. Her bangles chatter as she pins up more clothes, her red sari glowing behind Sujata's widow-white ones. Ankita thinks of the first time she got her period in India. She had been so humiliated because there were no laundry hampers or washing machines to throw her stained underwear into. She couldn't bear to hand them over to Aparna, who was a boisterous teenager back then, catching every opportunity to tease her. Ankita's mother showed her how to soak her soiled clothes in a bucket full of soapy water in the bathroom. As Ankita watched, hugging her knees to become as small as possible in shame, her mother tacked her underwear up in an unassuming corner of her grandmother's patio, next to the withering fig tree Ankita was always warned to steer clear of. Aparna's arching body takes the same shapes her mother's did then, fingernails catching the last bit of light as she releases each bright plastic clip on the line.

Ankita has a strange urge to do chores even though she loved lethargic summers in India as a child. She ate well and never had to clear the table, dozed in the afternoon, spent hours watching Hindi soaps she only half understood. Her mother was never content with this lifestyle. She flitted around the household help, picked fights with Sujata, shooed Ankita into the streets to play with her cousin who was much older and didn't know what to do with her. Ankita spent quiet evenings riding with her cousin on his bicycle around the alleyways of Dhakuria, sitting on the bike frame as he pedaled around potholes. He bought her ice cream and made her promise not to tell anyone when he bought loosies from the little shop on the corner. They shared content silences, Ankita eating ice cream on the curb while her cousin smoked by the ribbons of chip bags that framed the shop front.

After her mother's funeral, Ankita rotted on the couch like the trays of food left untouched for days in her parents' house. Even David let her sulk for weeks while he did all the chores around her. But now Ankita feels her mother's restlessness bestowed upon her from the grave. The walls induce a kind of panic. Ankita sees how a room can be oppressive, how idleness can be hypnotic.

While Sujata applies makeup at her vanity, Ankita asks tentatively, "Should I make tea? Since Aparna is busy with the laundry?"

"Aparna left," Sujata says, gaze focused on her own reflection. "It's a long way home, and her husband beats her senseless if she's not there by sundown."

"She's on the balcony."

"Still?" Sujata turns around, one eye lined, both concerned. She crosses the room to look out the window. "No, she's gone."

Ankita joins her, peering out the iron grate at the perpendicular wall. The balcony is vacant, the line of saris puffed with evening air. "Someone was there."

"She must have just left."

But Ankita hadn't heard the gate outside the threshold rattle, or the heavy front door slam shut. Sujata returns to her vanity, but Ankita lingers. *Ghosts are just memories*, she tells herself again, even as she searches for a flicker of red between the damp cloth.

"You've grown quiet," Sujata says while she and Ankita sit in traffic. "You remind me of your mother when she first came to live with us." They had all lived in that house when Ankita's grandmother was alive—Ankita's grandmother and her older sister, both widows; Sujata, her husband, and her son; Ankita's parents and eventually baby Ankita for the first few years of her life.

Ankita laughs. "Ma was never quiet." Her mother had been a preschool teacher and always talked like she was addressing a room full of rowdy children. Ankita wants to accuse her aunt of sarcasm, but doesn't know the right words in Bengali.

"She was when she was a new bride. My mother and aunt were hard on her. And she was far from home. She came to us from Lucknow, you know."

Ankita does know. She and her father were born here in Kolkata, but her mother came only after marriage. "Lucknow isn't far," Ankita says.

"Not compared to America. But it was to her back then."

They reach the market and leave the driver to park somewhere while they shop. Summer has the city slowly decomposing, thick with body odors and overripe fruit. Vendors press close to their sluggish fans and flap their saris in a futile attempt to stir the dense air. Shoppers pass between them in clumps of umbrellas and sweat-stained cotton. Some gather around cold drink and ice-cream stands for respite. Sujata navigates the cracked sidewalk with practiced finesse. The gold and jewelry stores stand in a glossy strip at one end of the street, glass walls promising cool air. Inside, Ankita stays mute, not wanting to reveal her foreign pockets.

The shop clerk tries several times to bring Ankita into the conversation, but she refuses. Sujata picks the simplest jewelry per

Ankita's earlier request. While her aunt haggles, Ankita, unneeded, wanders to the window.

Ankita's mother had kept her coral and conch bangles in a velvet box in her dresser. They were too fragile to wear every day, she told Ankita, who would sometimes secretly take them out while her mother was showering. Ankita would suck the candy-like rings and graze them with her teeth. But Ankita remembers her mother's gold bangle best, thick and shining on her wrist. She never took it off or let Ankita play with it the way she played with her mother's other jewelry. It was the most precious, she insisted. Taking it off was bad luck. The one night she left it at home, she and Ankita's father hit some railroad tracks on his motorbike. He almost lost a finger, and she almost lost Ankita in the womb.

She hasn't touched any of her mother's things since her death. Ankita has barely even set foot in her parents' bedroom. That box must still be there, still fragile, still shut away in the dark.

A woman stops in front of the window and leans against it, fanning herself with the cloth draped over her head. Ankita imagines that she's her mother, waiting just outside for them to come out and show her the new jewelry. Ankita trails her fingertip along the warm glass, following the line of the woman's spine. The woman turns her head just slightly and raises her arm as if to point. Ankita follows it with her gaze.

The woman's arm stretches out of her sari's hem and across the sidewalk, twisting around slow pedestrians. Ankita blinks, shakes her head, but nothing changes, and no one else takes notice. A man stands next to an ice-cream stand, smoking a cigarette. The woman's hand reaches past him and slides into the ice-cream cart while the vendor hands a Kwality cup to a little girl. She takes out an ice pop and traces its yellow wrapper on the man's neck, shoulders, behind his ear. He takes a long drag of his cigarette and shuts his eyes.

"Ankita." Sujata at the counter, paper box in hand. "Let's go."

They walk out together, Ankita clutching her aunt's sari like she's a child. She searches for the woman, but she's gone. The man continues to smoke alone, eyes closed.

Once home, Sujata pulls out old photos. They smell like the sandalwood from the box that kept them. While she sorts through, Ankita asks her father, "What was Ma like when she got married?"

"Depressed," he says in English, because Bengali isn't so clinical with sadness. "She didn't sleep at night for a long time, barely spoke during the day." He sighs. "The arrangement was very hasty. I wasn't her first choice, you know. Our fathers were old friends, but we'd only met a few times during the holidays. She liked some librarian who lived in her flat. I saw him once when I visited—handsome, a bit shy, but you could tell just by looking that he wasn't right for her— socially, I mean. Family in a different place. Anyway, her father found a Cadbury bar and some pressed flowers in one of her library books, and it all went quickly from there. Engagement, marriage. Suddenly she was in Kolkata with a man she hardly knew."

Ankita didn't know that marriages still happened like that. She always knew her parents were arranged, but that was true for almost anyone in their generation. She assumed theirs was like her cousins', with meetings and dates, chances for the two of them to get to know each other before they decided. She wonders what her mother's parents were like. Her mother was a rare only child, and Ankita's maternal grandparents had died while Ankita was still young. There were very few photos of them. Ankita knew her parents had known each other as children. She had imagined that one day, when they finally took note of each other's adulthood, they felt the same as she had when David leaned down to take a beer out of her friend's fridge, even before she knew his name—a shiver of anticipation in her flesh, something settling in her bones. It was strange to imagine her mother looking at a nameless, faceless man with the same sensation.

"We should have been kinder to her," Sujata says from where she sits cross-legged in front of the metal armoire. She sees the discomfort in Ankita's posture and knows it's time to change the subject. "Our mother gave her a really hard time."

"We were married for almost a year before your mother started to talk much at all, and then she had such a mouth. I loved it." Ankita's father laughs. "She wanted to work—even when she was pregnant—in that dingy schoolhouse for street kids. Your grandmother thought she was possessed."

"You can't blame her," Sujata says. "Your wife sat under that courtyard tree all evening, right next to the drain. And when she suddenly went from silent to loud and restless—that wasn't natural."

That shriveled laurel fig is in the tiny square patio outside the back door of her grandmother's house, enclosed on all sides by neighboring homes. Her mother told her to never touch it, in case it was diseased. It's been there since before Ankita's great-grandfather built the house. Its branches were always dry and twisted, fed rotten water from the open drain. She pictures her mother sitting on the warm stones, staring wistfully at it. "Why didn't anyone cut the tree down?" Ankita asks.

Her father scoffs. "My mother was a superstitious woman. She was convinced it would release some evil spirit."

Ankita understands this in a way. She was afraid of the tree even as she got older. Part of that fear came from the scary stories her grandmother told her, but there was something about the tree itself too. Sometimes when the light was just right, Ankita saw faces in its bark.

"Here." Sujata hands Ankita a photograph. "One of the only ones we have left." In a monsoon accident a month after their honeymoon, all her parents' wedding photos drowned when a window burst open while they were out. This small photo has rounded corners and a faded pastel image of Ankita's mother in a red wedding sari, a deep scowl under the white dots around her brow. Her hair was tied in a knot, tucked back under her veil, the matching lipstick turned pink with time. There are things she never told Ankita—things that Ankita never thought to ask. How much of what she knows about her mother is true, and how much is assumed? It feels lonely to wonder.

Sujata slides the red, gold, and milk-white bangles onto Ankita's wrist one by one. It should have been done when she was first married, but Ankita wanted a diamond, a white dress, and neither of her parents objected. Sujata's eyes begin to drip as the bangles slip back, clacking together at the softer part of Ankita's arm. Sujata pats her face with her sari and says, "We should have been kinder."

Before bed, Ankita video calls David. She shows off her bangles. He tells her they're beautiful.

"I wish I could've picked them with you," he says.

"I don't think you're supposed to be there for that anyway," Ankita replies, resting her arm in her lap.

"See? I don't know anything. I could've learned so much."

Ankita shrugs. "It's fine. It's not like I know much myself."

"We'll go again. We'll learn together."

"Sure." Ankita nods to appease him. Truthfully, she's not sure if she wants to. She doesn't feel like she fits in here any more than she felt she fit in with her white classmates in the earlier years of her school life, before she smoothed out all her foreignness. She's no longer a little girl who can eat ice cream on the curb and pretend she's like the other children just because she looks the part.

Ankita is on her grandmother's patio, squatting over the open drain to pee. She watches the sparse leaves rustle on the fig tree, and the tree stares back. *This is a dream*, Ankita realizes when the pee won't come out. She wakes to a strange silence. No stray dogs in heat, no cars or wind. A figure in red stands at the foot of her bed. Her sari is draped over her head, her face in shadow. Ankita is in her parents' teak wedding bed, surrounded by the mint walls of her grand-mother's house. She can't move. It has been years since she's had sleep paralysis, but she tries to stay calm and wake up. She wants to shut her eyes but can't. The figure crawls onto the bed. Out of the corner of Ankita's gaze, she watches her lean over David, asleep beside Ankita. The figure whispers something in his ear. Ankita strains to hear, but there's no sound.

Ankita wakes sweating. The room is bright, and the city is already bustling outside. She is in her aunt's apartment again, in an empty bed. The silver jar with her mother's ashes gleams like a sharp tooth on the dresser. Her father is stepping out of the shower when Ankita opens the bedroom door. "Can't we visit Amma's house? Just once?" she asks him as he towels off his hair.

"Why? It's not safe."

"Just to see it. It's been so long."

"That place isn't like you remember. It's better to just let it be."

"Please." Ankita's voice breaks. "I'm having nightmares. I keep thinking about Amma's stories. I need to see it."

Her father frowns and presses his cool knuckles to her forehead. "The heat is getting to you. Are you sure you want to come to the temple today?"

Ankita nods. She doesn't want to miss the only outing her father has invited her on so far.

"Take a cold shower," he says, skirting around her to get into the bedroom. "Have Aparna make you tea. You can get some sleep in the car."

Ankita runs on her toes toward the temple, terra-cotta tiles scorching her bare feet. Her father, ahead on the path, does a similar dance. A group of women standing along the shady edges laughs at them as they pass. The river comes up brown and white, nearly blinding. Ankita and her father dart off the path and descend the steps straight into the water, until they're ankle-deep.

"We should have checked our shoes." Her father sighs. They left their sandals in the car with the driver, who told them the same.

The stairs are crowded. A man beside Ankita dives smoothly into the water, and several women emerge just ahead of them, soaked saris clinging tight to their bodies.

"I could have just scattered them here."

"What?"

"Ma's ashes."

Ankita's father shakes his head. "I don't know why you brought them all the way here. There's no point now. It's past time to do any rites."

"But that's what she wanted." Her mother always said so when she was feeling dark or sentimental on winter evenings. In the days after she passed, Ankita could only think of acrid smog, the cool cement of her grandmother's house, this murky river. "Isn't there some ritual we could do?"

"There's a ceremony," her father says. "It costs money, and it should've been done within days of her cremation."

"I'll pay. I want to do it right."

"We'll talk about it later."

Ankita's mother loved this temple. She came alone every time they visited Kolkata. Ankita tries to imagine what her mother thought about the first time she saw this sacred river. It must have meant something to her.

"Did she love you?" Ankita asks her father suddenly, just as he's about to walk away. The question hangs for a while, almost swallowed by splashes and chatter, the distant clamor of rituals. Then her father laughs.

"I was her husband. Why are you asking me such an American question right now?"

Ankita looks at her submerged feet.

"Is this because of what I said last night? We left all of that behind. She was happy in the US. What is a couple chocolate bars compared to a life together? Come on; we don't have time for this."

They hop from straw mat to straw mat until they reach the main temple. A serpentine queue covers most of the sun-bleached court-yard. Throngs of worshippers stand or squat in wait, glistening with sweat. Ankita's father meets with a man who takes their bowl of fruits and sweets. He disappears into the altar through the back door and emerges a few minutes later to hand the offerings back. Ankita gets only a glimpse of the goddess—black arms and wild-eyed profile, red tongue. Ankita and her father light some incense.

Ankita's mother must have waited hours to kneel before the goddess and actually look into her eyes. She would return home flushed and press the knot in her sari to Ankita's forehead. Ankita looked forward to it because her mother always returned with her favorite sweets—the best ones were made at this temple.

Ankita waits at the entrance while her father calls the driver. Tired of standing in the sun, she sits on the steps in front of a shaded corridor of shops selling those sweets. As she watches her father talk, pace, then squint out toward the road, a hand comes in and strokes her jaw with its knuckles, leaves light touches on her ear. Ankita turns, but no one is there, only a long arm stretching out of the crowd with an offering: a milky gold disk no bigger than a sand dollar. Gleaming on the arm's wrist is her mother's gold bangle. Ankita takes the sweet, and the arm retracts, snaking back into the crowd. She searches every sari-clad woman for her mother's face, her gait. If not her mother, then who? She shivers and turns back to the river as she takes a bite of the sweet. A long black hair comes out between her teeth, cooked in like a prize ring.

"Ankita!" Her father approaches with her sandals dangling in one hand. She crams the rest of the sweet into her mouth, swallowing quickly before he reaches her.

In the car, he unwraps the banana leaves from their offerings and hands her an identical sweet. She taps it to her forehead, her chest, then presses it against her lips, but finds she has no appetite.

"Aren't they your favorite?" her father asks, watching expectantly.

She nods and forces it into her mouth.

At home, she vomits everything she ate that day. Her aunt blames the heat, her father the sweets. Unable to throw away the blessed food, Sujata eats a few despite her diabetes and sends the rest home with Aparna.

Ankita pays for a ceremony. Her aunt and father insist that it's unnecessary, but her mother had asked for very little besides this. Ankita finds comfort in pretending her mother can still care, fearing the indifferent silver jar that remains. Dressed in white, the family arrives at the riverside temple as early as they're allowed, before the crowds swarm the place. Morning colors the sky like chalk dust, smothered by pollution. The late-sleeping city is still subdued, the Bally Halt bridge a silent web in the distance. The priest speeds through the scripture, and Ankita recites back the Sanskrit clumsily, hands sweating around the cloth-wrapped urn with her mother's ashes. She sets them adrift in the river, and that's it—her mother is gone. Ankita stays at the riverbank for a long time, waiting for tears that don't come. At last, her father takes her by the shoulders. "Come on," he says, steering her away. "They need to start the next one."

On the ride home, Ankita is full of regret even though she has no idea what else she might have done with the ashes. She wishes she kept a little, a small vial, so some piece of her mother would remain with her. She doesn't dare say anything to her father or aunt, anticipating the *I told you so*. Instead she stares out the window, pressing her forehead to the warm glass. Kolkata is more forest than city. Ankita finds it beautiful, even the cement streaked with grime. Lush trees and vines drip from the colonial architecture, choking every building. She tries to guess if any of them are laurel figs, but she's not sure what that withered tree looks like when it's swollen with moisture and nutrients and life.

At Sujata's house, they eat lunch with the relatives who came to the ceremony. A group of aunts Ankita hardly remembers strokes her hair and admires her new bangles. The women ask about her husband, and Ankita's tongue loosens as she speaks, the innate draw of her first language prying open her jaw gently. She tells them he's kind and funny. A person who doesn't understand all of her but knows the best parts.

While Sujata is caught up in another conversation, Ankita asks two of her aunts, "Have you been to Amma's house recently?"

They exchange looks. "Not lately. It's locked up."

"Sanjoy says we'll fix it, make it modern," one adds, saying the word *modern* in English.

"Abhijit says we'll destroy it and sell the land," another says.

"I was thinking of going to see it."

"No!" They both gasp in unison. "You shouldn't go."

"Why not?" Ankita asks, reaching for a glass of water as an excuse to lean closer. Her aunts look uncomfortable.

"Even if it wasn't falling apart, that house is bad luck for young brides. Your mother had a bad time there. Sujata too when she and her husband lived there for a time. Your grandmother must have as well when she first arrived, because she was always going on about a spirit in the courtyard."

Ankita glances at Sujata sitting beside her, eating another sweet she's not supposed to touch. "I thought it was just a story."

"It's an old story," one of the other aunts says, leaning into their conversation. "Who knows? It's good to stay careful."

Sujata looks at Ankita, then turns wide-eyed and snatches the glass from her hand. "What are you doing?"

"Sorry, I forgot." Ankita stares at the tap water, the glass trembling in her aunt's plump fingers. "Where does it come from? The water."

"Ganga," Sujata says. "All the water in Kolkata is from there."

"And you drink it?" Ankita feels nauseated again, the too-big lyangcha she just ate churning in her stomach. The river full of rot and waste and the remains of dead Hindus. Not even fish can bear it.

Her aunts all laugh. "Look at your face," one says. "Our stomachs aren't coddled by American water. And it's filtered many, many times."

Embarrassed, Ankita breaks from the conversation and walks out onto the balcony. She leans her elbows on the stone railing. Dust sticks to the bottoms of her feet; Aparna hasn't had the chance to sweep yet.

In the unit on the opposite wing, a woman sits cross-legged at the threshold to the neighbor's balcony, just as Ankita imagines her mother sat before the courtyard tree. The woman's face is half-obscured by hanging laundry as she sinks her teeth into the purple wrapper of a Cadbury bar and chews it down, paper, foil, and all. Between bites she grins, taunting Ankita with a mouth caked in greasy chocolate like mud from the foul riverbed. *How stupid, how American, to think you could put me to rest just like that.*

That night Ankita and her father sit in front of the television after her aunt has gone to sleep, both reluctant to face their lingering jet lag in the too-stiff bed.

"Do you feel better?" her father asks, passing her the bag of Khatta Meetha he's been absently snacking on.

"Kind of." Ankita crunches a handful and adds carefully, "But I'd really feel better if I could see Amma's house."

"Why are you so fixated on that?" Her father turns down the volume on the TV. She and her father never talked like this before her mother's death. Heart-to-hearts between them were rare, her mother's strong presence eclipsing theirs. But lately they've been able to ask more of each other, to fill the space she left behind. Ankita shrugs.

"I don't know. I keep seeing Ma everywhere. I'm having weird dreams. Maybe I need it for closure."

"I know it's been hard. It's been a long time since you've been home."

Ankita places the snack bag on the coffee table and says, "This isn't my home." It's hard to admit, especially to her father.

He looks a little sad, but nods. "To be honest, I don't think it's mine anymore either."

Ankita feels a little bad then for wallowing in her own boredom and grief, resenting her father for leaving her with it. She is certain that he's suffering. It's possible that he is also, in his own way, trying to spare her from the same.

"Amma's house was home," she says quietly. The house where her father and his father grew up. Where she took her first steps. Where her mother found her voice. "I miss it. It feels wrong to leave without seeing it just once." Ankita doesn't tell him that when she leaves Kolkata this time, she won't be back. She suspects he already knows. The tears come quickly, now of all times, over the clashing cymbals of a Hindi serial soundtrack. She brings her legs up against her chest, wetting the knee skin against her cheek.

"Okay, okay." Her father rubs her back with his flat palm. "Don't cry anymore. It's done. We'll go."

Ankita is on her grandmother's patio again. The clotheslines streak in front of her, the dark house staring shuttered and asleep. Her mother kneels before her on the tiles, gazing up. She is young, with thick hair tucked behind small ears and plump cheeks. *What do you want from me?* she asks, and Ankita wants to tell her—*Nothing, everything, I don't know.*

I just want you, Ankita tries to say, but from her mouth comes a sound like a thousand insects, a summer downpour, the shaking

Puloma Ghosh

leaves of a dying tree that fades into a stray dog's eerie keen as Ankita
wakes in the dark once more.

The trip lasts only two weeks. Just as the jet lag begins to ebb, it's
time to leave. Ankita, her father, and Sujata drive to Dhakuria the
day before the flight. The house has been unoccupied and unkempt
there for years while the family argues about what to do with it.
From a back alley, it watched tall apartments and shopping malls
form around it.

This afternoon is the hottest yet, climbing past forty Celsius. The
three of them wait for nearly an hour in traffic until the streets
become familiar again. The mouth of the alley is one of the few
places unchanged from Ankita's memories. The lake beyond the
railroad tracks surrounded by shanties, the police station lined with
rusting shells of cars and bikes stripped of all their useful parts. The
electronics shop with kitchen appliances of decades past. The man
who irons clothes—undoubtedly the son of the one from Ankita's
childhood—smoking a cigarette in his stall.

The car is too wide to fit in the curved alley, which has a row of
houses on one side and a high stone wall on the other, separating it
from the shopping center on the main road. Sujata and Ankita leave
her father with the driver and walk on together. Trash lines the narrow passage, but the stray cats walking the wall are unexpectedly
white. Amma's house is the second one around the bend, golden yellow grayed out with grime. Sujata struggles with the verandah gate,
its heavy padlock jammed, hinges rusty. She pauses at the steps. "I

think I'll stay here. This place gives me a bad feeling. Are you sure you want to go?"

Ankita nods.

"Watch out for snakes." Sujata hands Ankita the keys and walks back into the alley to chat with a neighbor who greeted her as they turned the corner.

Ankita enters from the verandah through the dark, waiting doorway. Inside, the lights miraculously still work. The house emerges like a memory, cracked and veiled in cobwebs. Not even cockroaches or geckos inhabit it. A naked bulb lights the low-ceilinged hallway, the pale rectangle on the wall where the refrigerator had once been. Everywhere, the land encroaches, taking back what the house tried to press down. Vines snake in between shutter hinges. Her parents' room is without furniture, littered with decaying plant matter and fallen petals of mint-green paint and drywall. The bathroom floor has a large wound, termites busy in and around it. The wilderness left only the living room untouched. Remnants of her family are strewn about. Ankita recognizes some old toys, an ancient armoire looming in the corner, her grandparents' mahogany altar. Dusty murtis of her grandmother's favorite gods stand sentinel inside the altar with their round eyes and fat red mouths: the universe, its brother, its sister.

Ankita hears the gate to the patio open and shut. She walks carefully down the hallway, wondering if it's an intruder or maybe a snake. There's no one. The gate is locked. Ankita tries the keys one by one until it opens, hinges groaning. Sun-bleached clotheslines still crisscross the patio. Broken furniture and rotting leaves are littered about. The fig tree has overtaken the far wall, larger and stronger than Ankita has ever seen. It leans toward her. A woman crouches within its foliage, red sari fluttering.

"Ma?" Ankita calls. She reaches up to clutch the hem of the woman's sari, longing to see her mother's face the way it was when she was young—round and copper, a freshly minted coin.

"Ankita." The woman's voice is brittle, harsh. She lowers her head to reveal a knotted-wood face. It shifts, molding into different features as the leaves stir. Ankita steps back, and the woman laughs, a sound like snapping twigs. "Don't be afraid. You know me."

One of the branches twists forward. It's an arm, covered wrist to elbow with red, white, iron, and gold bangles. Its hand traces Ankita's ear tenderly. It smells like the inside of a velvet jewelry box, a sugary milk sweet, her mother's neck. The touch feels so familiar, Ankita leans into it, closes her eyes, and whispers, "I missed you."

"You don't have to anymore. I'll stay with you."

Ankita nods, opening her stinging eyes. Another hand emerges from the leaves and selects the white bangle closest to its wrist. The bangle slides off with unexpected ease. The woman offers it to Ankita, her grin revealing a row of sharp teeth. Ankita isn't scared. She's not sure if she ever was. The long arms, the pointed teeth behind pretty lips—they feel like they've always been part of her. How far she has to reach to find herself. How everything she tries to hold is sharp. She touches the bangle. It's creamy white like ivory. "What is it?"

The creature holds Ankita's wrist and gently slides the bangle on. "Your mother's bones."

"Are you satisfied?" Sujata asks as Anita shuts the verandah gate. Ankita turns around and offers the keys.

Sujata shoves the padlock shut. "Did you lock everything you opened?"

Ankita nods. She watches a group of neighborhood children chase one another barefoot through the alley. The soles of their feet smack the ground hard, unafraid.

Sujata takes Ankita's wrist as they walk back to the car. "You've already managed to get it dirty?" The white bangle is now dull and yellowed, scuffed in places.

"I'll clean it when I get home."

"Take care of it. Don't wear it all the time."

A light wind funnels between the stone and cement. The air carries the smell of sewage, sweat, and the fritters sold on the next block. If Ankita shuts her eyes, she can return to the afternoons on her cousin's bicycle, cheek stuck to his damp arm. But that was a long time ago now. The city has a new skin, as does she. She tugs her hand out of her aunt's grasp. For a moment, Ankita is her mother, smooth cheeks and high, stubborn chin, walking away from a city that is now closed to her, already a stranger.

Leaving Things

The brochures were clear: *If you encounter a wolf, do not try to approach. Make a slow retreat. Knock on the nearest door. Find shelter.*

This wolf was much smaller than the ones in the pictures, though—a fur-sheathed heap in the alley. Unmoving. At first I thought it was a large, injured dog. Maybe dead. Even though I'd seen all the reports of women being dragged off by malicious wolves, I couldn't help but stop. Before curfew began, I was a vet. In school they taught us that aggressive animals were driven by fear and hunger and pain. I wanted to believe there was some noble, professional reason I stepped out of the street, but after so many months inside, I was probably just bored. I left my bag of canned goods in the mouth of the alley and tiptoed toward the prone creature. I was already too close by the time my eyes adjusted. Long, thick tail. Paws bigger than my hands. Hot, heaving breath.

The wolf was alive. She panted, whimpered, and twitched her legs. Her snout, a smooth gradient of white to silver, pointed its glistening black nose straight at me. A swollen belly trembled between her legs, the size and shape of which I'd seen many times on pregnant dogs. I took a slow step back, hoping she would let me pass by without a fight. If she was in labor, I didn't want to interrupt. Suffering animals are dangerous; mothers even more so. I'd seen my own mother chase a one-night stand out of her house with a kitchen knife when he raised his voice at me over breakfast.

My second step skidded in the gravel, echoed a crunch between my small body and the beast's jaws. She opened her eyes, parted her lips, and whined. She scrabbled at the gravel but ultimately couldn't pull herself upright. She leaned up and stretched her neck toward me, her eyes catching the light from the street in a flash of amber. I recognized this look from all the wounded animals that had looked pitifully at me from the papered examination table. *Do something*, they said. *Make it stop.* And this is maybe why I became a vet, because of how tender this look made me. I remember first seeing it on my family's pet cat as he gazed at me in his last moments, asking me to end it. I was maybe nine. My mother knew the cat was dying, so she had wrapped him in a blanket and placed him in his favorite bed, waiting for him to let go. He slipped away slowly on a long, sleepless night. Overcome by that animal aversion to death, I couldn't touch him, and for years after, I'd wish I had.

I edged forward, and the wolf stilled. After all this isolation, I felt reckless. I had lost sight of what I had wanted to hold on to out here. So what if this was it? But she made no threatening gestures, even as I came within arm's length. I crouched. "Hey, girl," I whispered. The wolf prodded my shoe with the tip of her nose and licked it. Poised to jump back at the slightest movement, I reached for her. I placed a hand on her neck. She nudged my toes. I brought my fingers up to her face and let her smell me, and I was startled by how tame she was. She sniffed and touched my palm with her muzzle. It was velvety, wet at the edges of her mouth. "Stay here," I told her, and she blinked as if she understood me.

I returned to the corner store adjacent the alley. The shop's bell chimed as I walked in, and the man at the counter looked away from the staticky television nestled in between a cleaned-out cigarette display and obsolete lottery tickets. "Back so soon?"

"I forgot something."

I found the last box of oversized garbage bags in the half-empty shelves. Supplies had been scarce for some time; truckers were frightened to come through after countless traffic accidents and roadside attacks from roaming wolves. Shipping companies didn't want to be liable for employee injuries. We received what could come by air, but our local airport only landed tiny passenger planes and just a few flights during the blazing center of day. Everyone agreed that such a tiny city in the snowy edge of the country should be abandoned readily. The few of us left were the last holdouts.

"You shouldn't be walking around." The balding man scanned the box at the counter.

"I would have run out of food." My stockpile of canned vegetables, beans, and tuna was down to a single can of corn. I handed him my credit card.

"You could have sent someone else. Your boyfriend, father, brother . . ." He put on his reading glasses, which hung from his neck by a purple shoelace, and pulled his card reader from below the counter.

"I live alone."

The man shook his head without glancing up from the card reader as he swiped for a third time. "Sorry, this thing is a pain in the ass. People used to pay cash mostly, but now . . ." He trailed off. The ATMs had been empty for quite some time. His fourth try seemed to take. "Kids like you worry me," the man continued. "My daughter moved back home some time ago. Didn't want to risk it on her own." He handed the card back, and we both stared at the machine's dull olive screen. *Processing . . .*

The receipt printed at last, and I tucked the box under my arm.

"Hey." The man leaned over the counter so his head stuck out past the impulse rack. "Just so you know, we're leaving here in a month. You should too. Everyone will be gone soon."

I smiled. "I'll look into it." That was a lie. I had the means to leave, yes. A mother who would welcome me home until I could get back on my feet. But I hadn't told her yet that my boyfriend had left me, and it felt easier to stay where I was than make plans for a future I didn't want to think about yet. I just wanted to focus on the problem at hand.

Back in the alley, the wolf watched me shake open a garbage bag. "It'll just be a little while," I told her. "My apartment's right around the corner."

I was prepared for a struggle, but the wolf bowed her head to me. I slid the garbage bag on her slowly, trying not to catch her fur with my fingers. A fresh coat of snow clung to the sidewalks like new paint. I dragged her easily along it, leaving a smear of concrete and erasing the shoe prints that had brought me there.

In my apartment, I pulled off the garbage bag bit by bit and lay the she-wolf on the kitchen tiles. Her eyes were closed, her face still. I dug through her fur for a pulse, a heartbeat, but got nothing. I pressed my fingers deeper, hoping I'd missed it, but it was no use. My chest grew tight with either panic or grief, I couldn't tell which. I got on my knees, finding the widest part of her chest with the heel of my palm. I locked my fingers together and pressed quickly, counting in a hoarse whisper. After thirty, I tilted her snout back and took a deep breath, exhaling into her wet nose. Then I did it all over again. And again. Despite my knees getting scuffed on the kitchen tiles, I felt more like myself than I had in some time, useful at last. I could almost smell the antiseptic tang of the clinic. Hypnotized by the back-and-forth of hands, mouth, hands, mouth, I continued longer than I probably needed to. I didn't know how long she had been dead. At last, my arms aching, I sat back on my heels. As I wiped my hands on my pants, I realized they were wet, not from the wolf or my spit, but from the sheen of tears on my cheeks. For the first time in months, I held a living thing in my arms, and I had let her die.

I touched her stomach and wondered if the cubs were still alive, if I could still save something. I had delivered puppies before many times, but never wolf cubs, and never from a corpse. I decided it would be best to cut her open quickly so as to not lose the cubs too. Her stomach was so swollen, I assumed it was a litter of at least five. Maybe some would survive. I didn't know what I'd do with them afterward, but there wasn't time to think about that.

I rummaged through drawers for a knife. Things had been in disarray since Austin left. In every relationship there is a clean one and a messy one, because no two people are ever the same degree of either. I was the messy one. Without Austin to put things in their rightful place, the drawers of utensils became cluttered—spoons and forks and knives interlocked like they were holding one another.

I crouched with the first large knife I found, though I had no idea if it would be sharp enough. I rolled the wolf over onto her back and tried to determine where to slice. I had only performed Cesareans on dogs, but I had learned how to treat wildlife in school and expected that a wolf's anatomy was not that different. The mother being dead did, sadly, make the procedure easier. I envisioned where the womb would be and placed my hand on her abdomen, knife positioned to cut. I noticed her belly twitching then, and at first I thought maybe she was still alive. Something undulated within her, pushing against my palm. I pulled my hand back, and in its place her fur began to darken, blood spilling from inside. Tiny, sharp-nailed fingers pushed out of the seam. I stumbled back, the knife clattering to the tiles beside me. For nearly half an hour, I watched small limbs kick and tear out of the wolf's womb, teeth gnashing through her skin. At last, a human infant with open eyes reached for me through the carnage. Dazed, with my mouth and nose full of coin-edged blood scent, I stuck my hands into the shredded flesh. I grasped the slippery child under its arms and pulled it from what was left of the wolf's soft flesh. The baby's pink skin was slick with blood and amniotic fluid. It grasped my wrists so tightly I almost dropped it. It was a boy.

An umbilical cord spilled from the wolf's collapsed bowels, tethered to the boy by his navel. I placed him in my lap and sawed through the cord with my knife, which was even duller than I imagined. When the cord came apart at last, I stood to throw the knife into the sink. At my feet, the boy grabbed the severed cord and brought it to his mouth. He chewed and watched me. I didn't bother trying to take it away and instead picked the boy up and clasped him to my chest, cord and all, the first warm body I had held in months.

I've always known men to be leaving things. Like my father, who left when I was too young to remember why, and my brother, who left for the army and never came home. Like Austin, who left two months into the curfew that made me housebound. My calendar shifted each week as my appointments got pushed back and back and back until they were finally canceled and disappeared. Unoccupied, I spent my days on the living room carpet, counting the shadow stripes from our blinds. The number never stayed the same—the sun moved, the weather changed—so I started over every hour. I longed for my office: the uninterrupted daylight through the waiting-room windows; the clean fluorescence in the examination room; my stethoscope pressed to a fluttering heart. Finally, Austin returned home one evening and said, "The dealership is done for. I'm going south."

"What should I pack?" I asked, to which he replied, "Don't," and I knew it was his turn to become a leaving thing too. By then I had already felt the letting-go grow between us, how we talked less often and seldom touched. I realized when I saw his things in suitcases that I had expected this, maybe from the very beginning. One night I lay silent beside him, and the next night I lay silent alone. He took the car and told me I could take a Greyhound to my mother's, but I put off buying my ticket, and a week later, buses no longer stopped at our city. I couldn't imagine walking down the highway alone, trying to hitchhike, hoping someone would take me in before nightfall. I was too humiliated to call my mother to come get me, to admit to her that I had been left behind as well. So I decided to remain in my apartment, hoping this would pass, knowing deep down that it would not. My last days with Austin confirmed the suspicion I always held: I was born only to become my mother's silhouette against the oval window of our front door, watching another man walk away. That we would always be a little pathetic, exhausted yet unwilling to part with our empty rooms.

When the women began disappearing from our city, walking into the night and never returning home, it was called a crisis. Not leaving, but taking. The wolves appeared in the autumn; they came out of the tree line and began to pick us off. We noticed them lurking in corners and streaking between alleys in the quiet hours. At first they only hunted at night, and there were rumors of kidnappings or serial killings, but bodies were never found, and we began to suspect they were eaten after all. Soon the wolves grew in number, and brazen packs roamed the streets at the height of day. It was easy to draw a correlation. Animal control tried but failed to capture the wolves or drive them out. They seemed unusually smart. Bigger than average, more ferocious. Experts quickly assigned predators and prey. City officials told women not to go out under any circumstances. They concluded that perhaps there was something in our biology that made us more delicious, entirely edible. People began to vacate; starting with a few families, then in huge waves. The beasts multiplied. The women dwindled.

This baby was something else entirely, neither wolf nor human. He was far too chubby and emotive for a newborn. He didn't cry when I pried the umbilical cord from his little hand—he just cocked his head curiously. His teeth were fully grown in with prominent canines, his nails sharpened to little points. By all other accounts he looked like a human child. I bathed him with the spray nozzle in the kitchen sink, and each time the water came near his face, he laughed that squeaky baby laugh. He had deep gold eyes like the she-wolf still lying dead on the tiles, slowly emptying of blood. I dried him off and tried to swaddle him in a fresh towel, but he squealed and kicked his feet out before I could wrap him well. I sat with him loosely bundled on the couch.

"Where did you come from?" I asked, and he smiled, unnerving fangs bared. I had no idea what to do with him. Would it make sense to take him to a human hospital or an animal one? I wondered if I would face any consequences for engaging with a wolf, even bringing it into my home—one unit in a building of many. There would be so many questions. Hours at the police station, no doubt. I didn't know how I would explain any of this or if they would believe me. What they would do with me afterward. Very little was known about why the wolves came or how long they would stay. As the months wore on, the city surrendered to them. In some ways, it made sense that the diminished northern woods would lash out at us with violence. Everyone silently agreed that to fight back was more trouble than this little city was worth.

I decided I would keep the baby. Not out of love or some misplaced desire for motherhood—I'd known for a long time that I never wanted to be a mother—but because it was more trouble to do anything else. If the wolf situation somehow turned around, maybe I could turn the boy in to the authorities, a university, whoever could make sense of him. *Look what I found after you all fled.* And if it didn't, maybe the wolf-boy could help me survive here. Maybe his big teeth and sharp claws could protect me if I played this right. And if he turned on me? Well, anything was better than returning, defeated, to my mother's doorstep and reoccupying the tacky bedroom I had left behind. I had almost no money left; I had maxed out my cards and was an inch away from defaulting on my vet-school loans. I chipped at my remaining savings with every trip to the convenience store. Every day it felt like dying inside a wolf's jaws was inevitable, even favorable. Sometimes when the night pulsed with wolves' cries, I wanted to walk right out and put an end to it. I didn't have it in me, of course. My blankets were too warm, and I would fall asleep, wake up again to the same bed.

What did a wolf-child eat? He was already too big to subsist on milk but too small to eat anything else. I thought about all the puppy diets I'd recommended in my life and wondered if there was any kibble left at the convenience store. Or was he better off eating baby food? I was curious whether he would grow into a human or an animal. I left the boy on the carpet, flanked by couch cushions, and set out, walking past the gory mess in the kitchen. I had always found ways to put off cleaning, and Austin wasn't there to give me shit. I wanted to do the exact opposite of what he would have done, just to prove he wasn't coming back.

Not far from my house, a patrolman turned the corner—he was part of the citizen watches that cropped up in the neighborhood among the diehards who refused to leave. The bat he swung was meant for wolves but looked menacing all the same. I ducked quickly into the nearest alley and waited for him to pass. From the alley's depths came snuffling, shuffling paws. Just after Austin had left, I'd made a few attempts to wander outside. I thought fresh air would clear my head, and I wanted to acclimate to taking care of myself. Each time, I was quickly collected and escorted home by a patrolman or frightened back by the silhouette of a wolf loping into the street not far from me. These days I only left out of necessity, and it was rare for me to do so twice in one day. I scurried carefully between my human and animal adversaries, praying that each corner I turned would reveal an empty street.

The shopkeeper was bewildered when I returned. "I'm sorry," I told him. "I keep forgetting things."

I scanned the shelves for baby or puppy food, but there was none. Instead, I grabbed cans of whatever I thought a baby might eat: potatoes, carrots, peas. Things I could mush up and shove into his waiting mouth. He did have teeth, so I bought some crackers too.

"Are you *sure* you don't need anything else?" the man asked as we waited for the card reader once more.

"Yes," I said, though I really didn't know.

"Hurry home, now. It's getting dark."

Cool tones coated my walk back. It was all but night, the sky a deep gemstone blue that faded quickly to black over the eastern rooftops. The streetlamps turned on. A few buildings from mine, the howls began. Some came from deep in the shadows of nearby alleys, very close to where I was. I sprinted the rest of the way, looking back only when my key was safely in the doorknob. The moon hung impossibly large behind me, round as a frosted cake.

Inside, the cushions were askew and the boy was gone. I searched under the couch, in the bathroom. My bedroom door was shut, but

I checked in there anyway. At last I stepped reluctantly into my little hallway-like kitchen. The boy was on his hands and knees, tearing bits of flesh from the wolf's open womb and eating it. I dropped my bag of cans with a resounding clatter. The boy looked up at me and smiled as if to say, *Welcome home.*

All the nearby farms and slaughterhouses were emptied for the season, ravaged by the insatiable wolves, and the city hadn't received any meat or fresh produce in weeks. I had no choice. I dug out the whetstone Austin bought when we first moved in. We had rarely used it, but now I scraped sharp every good knife we had. Surgery was not the same as butchery, but how different could they be? At the end of the day, it was cutting meat. I watched YouTube tutorials of men in jumpsuits skinning wolves, then attempted the ordeal myself. Skin doesn't separate easily from the body. It takes willpower. The process reminded me of my mother cutting fish in the sink when I was young. It was always cheaper to buy them whole, so she scraped away the scales herself, became deft at filleting with a thin, curved knife.

"I'll teach you someday," she told me when I came to watch, my elbows on the counter beside her. She never did. After I decided to be a vet, she stopped cooking meat and fish when I came home. I insisted that I wasn't vegetarian, but she refused anyway. I think it made her sorry to see our four hands on the table at dinner, my healing fingers next to hers fresh with death.

It felt wasteful to throw out the wolf's soft, thick pelt, but I had no idea what I'd do with it. If I kept it around much longer, my apartment would never lose the smell. I stuffed fistfuls of fur into a garbage bag.

There were no videos that demonstrated the best way to butcher a wolf or even a dog. I looked up some for pigs, but I wasn't sure if they would work the same way. I tried to chop off the limbs like I had seen the butcher do at the grocer's, but my kitchen cleaver hit thick bone and stuck there, the handle breaking off and leaving a neat rectangle of blade lodged in the joint. I left it in and went about painstakingly carving the meat off the bones and shoving them into freezer bags. For the bigger pieces, I used more garbage bags. The boy watched me from the threshold, babbling occasionally. When he started to cry, I sliced off a strip of raw meat and threw it over, and this appeased him for a time. Finally, when my freezer brimmed with packaged chunks of wolf meat, I rolled the carcass into a garbage bag. It was already dawn then, and the howling was more infrequent, farther away, so I slipped quickly out the side door to shove the bags of wolf remains into my bins.

When I came back inside, the smell hit me fiercely. It was amazing that I had gone so many hours without noticing it. I was certain it had seeped deep into my clothes, my hair. I ducked into the bathroom to throw up.

I found the boy asleep on the kitchen tiles. I fetched his towel and gently wrapped him up. I gathered every other rag and towel in my house to mop the blood smeared and splattered on every surface of my narrow kitchen. I prepared three batches of bleach solution, which I dumped each time the water began taking on a murky rust color. Some stains refused to come off, leaving brown marks on my cabinets. The boy was awake by the time I finished. Day bathed the kitchen in new light.

We showered together, me lying slumped against the slanted end of the bathtub while he sat between my legs and splashed in the shallow water, delighted. When the water started to run cold, I first dried off him, then myself with the last fresh towel I had. I left him to start a load of laundry, and when I returned, he was upright with his hands gripping the bathtub, shit smeared from the floor to where he stood, bouncing. I was so tired I wanted to kill him then, actually fantasized about slamming his little head against the rim of the bathtub. Nobody would know.

Instead I threw up again, mostly highlighter-yellow bile, and bathed him one more time. I used the towel to mop up his shit and threw it in the already running washer. To make a tight, thick-layered diaper, I ripped apart a few of the T-shirts Austin had left behind. Finally, the boy and I went to bed. He fell asleep quickly against my chest, and I held him close, pressing my face into his head. Ashy down was already growing out of his scalp.

I had held babies a few times before—children of neighbors and friends. I had grown up in a small town about a day's drive away from the little city I was in. Some of my classmates had children while we were still in school. They worked at the local restaurants and diners and inns, living off the small batches of tourists who came to vacation near the lake. The bookish ones completed online degrees so they could work at the bank or town hall or local schools.

The tougher ones drove trucks and worked on farms and factories down the highway. Some worked hard for scholarships so they could leave and never come back, like me. Some drank a little too much or got into drugs when they were bored or overworked, but that's true anywhere. Parents passed; children replaced them. That's how life in most places continues.

I always felt like the odd one. I was sad often. Maybe this was because of my father or my mother, or the books I read or the songs I listened to, but for my whole adolescence, my insides squirmed. Threatened to pour restlessness out of my mouth and ears. I couldn't stand the way my mother went to the same two jobs, the same couch, the same television programs each day. It seemed like some kind of hypnosis. That's how Austin found me. In class we sat together and convinced ourselves we were better than the people around us. He had sandy hair that was graying fast at his temples, even at seventeen, and an aspirational, patchy half beard that smelled like cigarettes. He wore shorts year-round, claiming that his abundant leg hair kept him warm enough. We took his truck out by the lake and moaned between bird and fox sounds. He told me words I'd wanted to hear all my life: *You're too good for this place* and *Let's leave together.* So we did.

I earned a scholarship to a university in this city, and Austin had a job at a car dealership. We found the perfect little apartment to lease, with a small but sunlit kitchen. My mother cried a lot when I told her I was leaving, but I was determined to not leave her even when I left our town. I called often, visited occasionally. I sent her gifts whenever I had extra money—chocolate-covered nuts, hard-cover books, glass jars of spices, wildflowers. I always showed up on her birthday and Mother's Day to make her lunch. When she asked Austin about grandchildren, he smiled at me and said, "Soon enough," because I still hadn't told him I didn't want any. I thought we were happy, until the wolves came.

The boy didn't have the milk-and-powder baby scent I expected. He smelled like the first dog I euthanized: a shaggy old mutt whose stomach had twisted in a way we couldn't undo. He was found lying abandoned in a park. Whoever had him before didn't want to be part of his passing. I was alone in the examination room when I injected him. He whined on the paper-clad table. I wrapped an arm around him and pressed my face into his fur as he drifted off. He smelled like dirt and pollen and carnivore. Like my mother's hands beside a plate of steak.

Every morning I woke up and found the boy had grown a little more. In days he was walking about, pressing his face against the window. When he got tall enough, I started to dress him in Austin's old T-shirts. The hem crawled from his ankles to his shins to his knees in maybe a week, which was also about how long it took for him to be out of diapers after a few days of watching me curiously while I sat on the toilet. I fed him raw wolf meat every day, but he never fussed. We sat together on the kitchen floor, his plated slab of meat and my bowl of canned fish with soggy, graying vegetables between us. He never once hurt me. I grew accustomed to his big teeth. His nails were all right when he wasn't shredding the carpet with them. I found a bag of cat toys and a scratching post left next to the bins behind my building. It seemed like a neighbor had recently lost their pet. I tried not to think about whether I could have saved it. Unless it was eaten, of course, somewhere out in the hostile streets. I brought home the toys and washed them as best I could. The boy loved every one.

I couldn't offer him much else. The toys I found online were far too expensive, with no guarantee that they'd be delivered. I made rattles using empty cans and bottle caps. The first time he hit his head on the table's edge, I went around taping socks to every sharp corner. I read lots of DIY mommy blogs after that, though none had any advice on how to cope with a child who grew at his rate.

At night he leaned out of my bedroom window and howled along with the wolves outside, the sound far bigger than his mouth and lungs. I tried to teach him words. *Sun. Sky. Floor. Bath. Meat. Me. You.* He never mimicked me, so I began to wonder if he would ever talk or just growl and howl.

One day I came home from the store to find the boy sitting cross-legged in front of the television. He had transformed from baby to child at that point and had a full head of gray hair in a haphazard style I'd cut myself. He smiled and said in clear English, "What's your name?"

Once he began talking, question after question spilled from him. We began to eat at the dinner table, and he'd go on incessantly throughout every meal.

"Where are we?"

"What is this?"

"Do we have anything else to eat?"

"Can I go outside?"

Eventually I relinquished my laptop to him, and he spent days hunched over the screen, searching and searching and searching—for what, I didn't know. I never taught him to read, but one morning I found him lying on his stomach, squinting intensely at a long, dense news article about our town's wolf invasion.

For a week and a half, he was a teenager. He didn't like to talk to me much then. He brought the laptop to the dinner table and typed and scrolled while we ate. He asked for bigger and bigger portions of meat. He no longer wanted to sleep in my bed, so I set up our air mattress in the living room. Sometimes, to my bewilderment, he left the laptop to work out, running around the apartment, doing push-ups, jumping jacks, and other exercises I couldn't name.

I laughed at him once. "Should I take you on a walk?"

He looked up, face shining with sweat, and said, "Yeah, actually."

I didn't, of course, and he refused to speak to me for the rest of the day.

After a few days of this, I was back to counting shadow stripes. Frustrated, I searched in the linen closet for some old board games Austin and I had—Scrabble, The Game of Life, checkers, Sorry!, Monopoly. I could tell he was annoyed when I asked him to look away from the screen and play with me.

"There's no point to these games," he said while I unfolded cardboard and dealt paper money.

"The point is to spend time with each other," I said, showing him my open palm full of little plastic pieces.

"We're always together," he retorted, though he picked a piece regardless. Cheekbones had begun pushing out of his face. He had a pointed nose and thin lips, round eyes. Even his human features carried traces of his mother.

He thought The Game of Life was silliest. "It's all chance. Life isn't just chance. Don't people do things on purpose?"

"You'd be surprised how much luck plays into it. The hand you're dealt."

"I don't think I'd find that surprising," he muttered.

"It's just a game." I flicked the spinner. My piece landed on *Job Search*. The card I drew read *Veterinarian*. I showed it to the boy, and he laughed. He handed me a tiny blue person—round head, square body, peg sticking out of its lower half. "Here. For accuracy."

Each of our game pieces was a little car with a stand-in for ourselves, our spouses, and our children stuck into tiny holes like pins. I smiled and placed his blue piece behind the pink one in my car.

"No." The boy picked up the piece and moved it to the front hole beside my pink piece. "If we ever drove anywhere, I'd want to sit in front." He flicked the spinner. I looked away.

I never let him go outside. I felt strongly that keeping him inside would keep him tame. Even once he was big enough to go to the store with me, if not on his own, I refused to let him. I told him it was because I didn't want people asking questions about where he came from. "They might separate us," I told him. "Take you away."

But really, the way he howled unsettled me, reminded me that no matter how many words he learned, he was still a beast. He moved with a strange, fluid grace, the way a quadruped slides its weight from flank to front foot. His voice had a grain to it like it could, at any minute, crumble into a growl. In his sleep he panted and shuffled his limbs like a dog dreaming of a hunt. I didn't want him to realize that he was a wild thing in captivity. It would be fine if he killed me, ate me the way he ate his mother piece by piece every day, but I had grown fond of him, his toothy smile and the way he had grown wit like it was something innate. Being with him was the easiest thing I'd done in a long time. I was his whole world since birth. If he still left me, it would prove once again that there was something deeply and irreparably wrong with me.

I installed a slide lock that closed the door from the front steps and a padlock for the inside. I kept the keys on a chain around my neck. He eyed them sometimes, and I began to wear high-neck shirts and dresses, hoping he might forget.

The boy stopped howling at night. Instead he masturbated a lot. I peeked out my bedroom door once to find him lying across the air mattress with his dollar-store boxers pulled off his hip, his face flickering blue in the laptop screen's light. His eyes were blank, lips only slightly parted, a thick black line into his mouth. Some nights I sat awake against the door, listening for the swipe of tissue being pulled from a box, his fingers returning to his keyboard. I tried to remember why Austin had stopped loving me. Was it something on my body, something inside my mouth, lodged between my teeth? After curfew, my idleness repulsed him. *How long have you been there? Did you ever move? What do you do all day?* These were the kinds of questions Austin had asked me.

If at seventeen, lying naked on his truck bed, exposed to a summer night thrumming with insects, I had said, *Let's stay. Let's live in my mother's house and have a baby. I'll work at the bank. You work at a bar. We can be happy here*, would he have gone sooner?

Who was I to think I was better than my mother? The little apartment Austin and I had was no different from the place we had left. We still went to our jobs, came home, and made dinner. We still had just a few rooms to call our own, a few friends to spend the weekends with. The hypnosis I feared had me in its chokehold before the wolves arrived. There is so little distinction between people's lives. Like my father, like the trail of men who came after him, Austin left too. It was predetermined in everything my mother passed down to me: her long eyebrows, her downturned nose, her wide lips. I wondered what the wolf-boy's mother passed down to him.

One morning he asked, "What are you listening for at night?"

"What?" I asked. I was in the middle of cooking some canned beans.

"I can smell you. Behind the door."

I turned away from the stove. The person in the kitchen entrance was tall. His gray hair fell past his ears since he had not let me cut it through his teenage days. Those days were behind him. His ankles and wrists peeked out from Austin's hemlines. His bare feet were enormous, even for his height, and curved into pointed toenails at their ends. Not a boy, but a man. I had done something unprecedented—the first vet to turn an animal so nearly human with their care.

"For the wolves," I told him.

"You can hear them through your bedroom window," he said.

"You used to howl." I wanted to change the subject. "Why did you stop?"

He stepped closer and placed one clawed hand on the counter beside the stove. "If I howl, they'll come for me. They used to gather in the street outside whenever they heard my voice. That's why I stopped."

I placed my spoon on the counter. "Would you go with them?"

"Would you?"

The beans sputtered.

"I think they're done," he said, pointing.

I turned off the stove and pulled a thawing bag of meat from the fridge. I took out my favorite big, sharp knife and tried to slice off a breakfast portion on the cutting board. The knife got stuck in the middle, where the meat was still frozen. It had long lost its ruby luster and was now a gray hunk freezer-burned on all sides. The man came behind me and said, "Here."

He placed his hands on mine and pressed. The frozen meat slowly gave way to the blade. His breath, just by my ear, caught as he pushed. His fingers were now twice the size of mine, truly lethal.

The knife hit the cutting board with a dull sound, but he didn't move right away. He pressed his nose behind my ear. "Don't you ever want to go somewhere else?" he asked.

"Why would I? You're here." I woke every morning finding it remarkable just to have a body in the same space as me. Every cough or yawn, the trickle of his piss in the toilet—all of it comforted me. He moved his head, and his lips touched the curved side of my neck lightly. I tightened my grip on the knife and closed my eyes.

He pulled away then, and I was surprised by my disappointment. While in isolation, my appetite for intimacy had swelled to a nonsensical degree. He, now a full-grown man, was the only other body near me, always moving about in my peripheral vision. As we ate breakfast, I imagined every part of him inside my mouth, how each one might taste.

Loving has many configurations. With Austin it was first his lips, then his wit, then the egg shape of his closed eyes. His tongue, his laugh, his favorite winter boots that he left behind when he went south. No longer needed, like me. The wolf-man seemed to have clawed his way out of his mother's stomach just to be a thing I could love. A homegrown rebound. We played games and watched action films that always ended happily even after many people died. He spent so much time reading about the world, knowing that the day of our departure was inevitable. He rarely touched fiction, except when I read out loud my favorite passages from novels, lying on the carpet with my feet up on his air mattress. I stopped watching the local news every night, stopped waiting for someone to tell me the curfew was over. A new hypnosis took over, and I sank into it gratefully, relieved.

One day as I grabbed more things from the convenience store, the shopkeeper handed me two shopping baskets of food and toiletries. "I'm leaving in a few days," he said. "This is all I have left in stock. It's yours, no charge."

"Can you really give this to me?" I asked, eyeing the baskets piled high. This explained how empty the shelves were, more so than I'd ever seen them.

"To be honest," he said, "you're the only one who comes around anymore. Almost everyone is gone."

I had noticed too that there were fewer and fewer patrolmen in the streets. On this trip I had encountered none.

"Oh. Well, thank you, then." I moved to grab the two baskets, and the man put a hand on my wrist.

"Listen." He placed his elbows on the counter and leaned closer. "Come with us. My wife and I worry about you. What will you do when you run out of this supply? We have a car. My daughter is about your age, good company. We can drive you wherever you need."

I slid the baskets off the counter, my hands out of his reach. "That's very generous, but I can't go. I'm needed here."

"For what?"

"Thank you so much for your kindness. It means a lot."

I walked home smiling. I took frequent breaks to set down the heavy baskets, but this was no problem because there was nobody to shoo me home. I no longer had to leave the apartment. Our small life was enough.

A few days later, about a month after the man was born, the lights went out in the apartment. I called ConEd, but they heard my zip code and told me they'd been instructed to cease services. "You should have been notified of evacuation."

I looked at the phone I hadn't touched in ages, the TV that had been on the DVD input for over a week. "Right," I told them. "Thank you, then." I hung up.

"Did you know that there was an evacuation order?" I asked the man, who was lounging with his legs spread on the couch, the laptop on his knees.

"Yeah," he said. "But I didn't think you'd want to leave." He wasn't looking at me, and it felt like he had done this on purpose, to punish me.

"Well, if they shut off the gas and water too, we're fucked."

He stood up and came close. Towering above me, he held my elbows and asked, "Do you want to leave, then?"

"We have nowhere to go."

"Your mother has been calling. And calling and calling and calling. And messaging. And emailing."

"That's private."

He laughed, sharp mouth bared at me fully like a warning. "In these little rooms? Please."

He didn't talk to me after that. He spent the rest of the day sleeping fitfully on the couch, waking sometimes to stare wide-eyed at the ceiling, then drifting off again. I dragged him from the couch in the evening, after it had gotten dark. We sat at the dinner table in candlelight, the light outside looking silvery bright in this new complete darkness.

"I feel strange," the man told me, picking at the meat on the table.

"Strange how?"

He set down his fork. "I've tried my best to be like you, but I'm not. Today I feel more different than ever."

I glanced at his claws. "Different how?"

He looked at me, his eyes clocking every fleshy bit—cheek, shoulder, breast. "I think you should lock your door tonight."

I reached for him across the table. "I'm not afraid of you. You love me, right? We are happy, right? Let's leave, then, like you've always wanted. We can be happy somewhere else too." I grasped his fingers. If I locked my door tonight, would he finally break down the front door, leap out the window?

He took his hands from mine and tucked them under the table. "I just want you to be safe."

As I washed the dishes, I noticed that the moon was full. It was incredible how much light it glanced onto us with its open face. No wonder I hardly noticed the snuffed streetlamps. The man came into the kitchen as I was drying my hands and asked me again to go into my room. As we said good night, I held on to him, wrapped my hands all the way around his broad chest so I could lock my fingers behind his back. I rested my cheek on his collarbones. I felt certain that this was it, the end.

I waited by the bedroom door, awake and listening when the howls began. I heard him stirring on the other side, grunting and making animal sounds I'd never heard from him before. At last I heard a scuffle, then the door rattled as his body slammed against it. My heart raced.

He whimpered on the other side and clawed the wooden doorframe. Paint chips sprinkled underneath. I thought of every animal I saw in the waiting room of our vet clinic, whining and struggling inside metal bars and mesh enclosures, how I longed to let them muck about the quiet room between our legs. I unlocked the door.

The man burst in as soon as the knob turned and held me just as I had held him before we parted. He licked my neck and tugged at my clothing with his teeth. I felt his erection against my stomach, and immediately my hands were between us, pulling away any fabric. The dreamy monotony of our life together tore away then. Sex, after so long and at its best, was something that snapped you wide awake to the world. His teeth became sharp on my skin, and when he chewed on my bare shoulders, the pain gave me a clarity I had tried so hard to smother. Just as I made him more human in our cohabitation, he made me more animal. His skin, rubbing my back and behind my knees, turned to the pelt I tore from his mother. His nails on my hips and back and chest. I bled everywhere. He clawed his way inside me the same way he clawed out into the world, and I leaned into it, longing to let all of my writhing insides spill forth at last.

When I woke it was daylight. I must have passed out, though I wasn't sure if it was from pain or the aftermath of pleasure. All my wounds were bandaged, and the man lay beside me, looking more human than I'd ever seen him. His nails were square tipped, his chest with only a thin layer of hair. "Good morning," he said. He rolled over and held me close.

I pressed my face into his neck and inhaled. He smelled freshly showered. "Are you going to leave now?" I asked.

"Are you?"

By afternoon his sharp nails were on my fingers. My mouth felt full of metal, but one swipe of my tongue told me they were my teeth, big and pointed. The trail from my pubic hair had extended up my stomach and chest; my arm and leg hair grew thicker. I didn't want to get out of bed, so the man brought me lunch on a tray I didn't know we had. A bowl of black beans and boxed rice for himself, a scrap of reheated meat for me. I chewed it down. It was sweet and juicy with the chemical aftertaste of freezer. When my plate was clean, I turned to him pitifully and asked, "What have you done to me?"

He kissed my forehead and said, "You opened the door."

All day I tried things. I tried to read, but the words blurred together. I tried to call my mother, but my phone was dead, with no electricity to replenish it. I tried to journal, but the pen kept slipping from my grip. I was hot and impatient. Feverish. I slept for most of the day except once, when I tore through the apartment looking for the man. I found him on the air mattress and pinned him down, bit his neck while he was inside me. When we finished, the air mattress was punctured and deflating. Satisfied, I stumbled into the kitchen to scrounge for more meat. The man helped me pull it out of the bag—my fingers were swelling and coming together, which made everything difficult to grasp. Ice chips clung to the meat like barnacles, but I ate it cold on the tiles, numbing my mouth.

I fell asleep as soon as my stomach was full, and later, I woke on the kitchen tiles, staring at the brown bloodstains I never could wash off. My paws facing the cabinets, my back against the oven. My ears twitching toward the window. The moon was no longer full, but almost so. It was bloated and pockmarked, just a dent filed off its side. The town outside dripped long, echoing cries. I rested my paws on the windowsill, pushed my nose against the glass. It smelled like wet earth and dirty concrete and something else I caught in the air for the first time.

The man appeared in the kitchen doorway for a minute. I smelled him there, soap and sweat. By the time I turned, I only caught the flash of my necklace of keys, dangling from his closed fist as he walked away. He wasn't in the hallway—only the open door. Small flakes drifted in. I stepped outside and saw eyes glinting in every shadow, beckoning. The night invited me in a way it never had before. My new body was swift and dense. The fresh snow soothed my paws. Wolves spilled out into the street, and we called to each other, the last breath of winter decadent in our mouths.

K

K appears as always, around midnight, a silhouette on my ex-roommate's stripped bed. Outside, the window is chewable black, broken only by the pinprick of the groundskeeper's porch light. The rest of my room is still: two wardrobes at the foot of my bed; two desks, one cluttered, one bare; the padlocked maintenance hatch on the ceiling. I know it's snowing because of the silence.

"Good night, K," I say, hoping it will make her disappear, but she remains there, sitting upright until my eyes close. She visits my dreams as a full-fleshed girl. She crawls into my bed and wraps her arms around me. Her face is round and dewy, doe eyes under overgrown bangs. "Isn't it better to sleep this way?" she asks, resting her head on my chest.

"Yes," I say, holding her close. It feels like she belongs only to me, like a lover or a child, even though the whole campus takes ownership of her, our K, our ghost. Throughout the years, many people have disappeared from this little mountain town. The incidents go back far longer than a single person's life span, and the victims have nothing in common. The theories are endless: alien abduction, portals to other worlds, unconfirmed rumors of occult activity. No bodies are ever found. The only university student counted among the missing is K, an orphaned photography major who disappeared one winter, leaving behind her belongings in the dorm room where I now sleep. Like all freshmen, I learned of K during orientation, sitting on the main lawn with a blanket between our bare legs and the ticks, listening to our orientation leader's last words of advice. My OL, Anya, was unbearably cool—short platinum hair, heavy eyeliner, tight black clothes. She leaned close and asked, "Are any of you in Lewis 309?" I raised my hand, and she fixed her foggy eyes on me with a smirk. "Watch out. That's K's room."

From then on, we noticed that K came up often in conversation like an inside joke. If a door closed by itself or a book slipped off a table, someone would ask, "Is that you, K?" That initial ricocheted through campus like an invocation even though nobody had actually seen her, not like I have.

Not long into first semester, my roommate swallowed a bottle of sleeping pills and went to the ER, then home, and that's when K began to appear at night—mirroring me on the other bed, a petite silhouette who refuses to fade no matter how much I blink.

We cohabit like this for a couple months, me half convinced that she is harmless, formless, maybe only a story I tell myself and others during the day.

Soon it's December, and I wake before my alarm to an unnatural chill. My blanket is cold all the way through from the air coming in the window adjacent my bed. I reach my stiff fingers to my phone, finding notification after notification from the campus alerts. The heat went out in Lewis at some point last night or early morning. Should be fixed by lunch. Dining hall opened early for the students to keep warm.

Outside, the season's first snow falls over a desaturated landscape—white field, spindly grove of bare trees beyond it, cloud-choked sky. In moments like this, when the world turns over in the span of one night, I feel something shift inside me too, a little click. The gauzy light reveals the impression of a body on the plastic mattress that once belonged to my roommate. I press my palm to it and find it warm. I pull my hand back quickly. Someone my shape and size has slept here.

Nobody believes that I've seen K's ghost in my room. Why should they? I'm a liar. It doesn't take long for people to realize that the stories I tell about myself are outlandish and contradictory. I have many people I talk to but none I consider a friend. They're always willing to be entertained, but otherwise keep their distance. I'm accustomed to this by now and understand that everyone feels uneasy around a person they can never truly know. Still, I can't resist the way my stories light them up, like they're children cross-legged on a library rug.

In elementary school, I was sent home again and again for lying elaborately. My father and stepmother didn't like the idea of sending a child to a psychiatrist, so my teachers compromised by setting me up with the counselor we had at school. Once a week, when my classmates went off to play, I had to take my lunch in Mr. Goodson's office instead. I resented my parents for this because I felt that they had started it by inventing my mother. She died in her early twenties, of what my father would never say, no matter how often I asked. I was a baby when she died, and I remembered nothing about her. It was obvious to me that she never existed. I was sure that one morning my father had plucked me from his garden.

Despite this, I liked Mr. Goodson. He was young, with smooth hair and big, straight teeth. He may have been the first man I was attracted to. I liked to watch his lips twitch and pucker as I spun one of my yarns, knowing full well that he didn't believe a word. I wanted to reach my little fingers into his mouth and feel his molars, tap his incisors with my fingernails. I tried to tell him many kinds of stories, hoping one might impress him.

"Kara," he stopped me as I described how my fingertips were fake, burned off and replaced with synthetic ones that tasted like fruit. "Is this true?" he asked.

"Of course not," I said, watching my classmates play four square on the blacktop outside his window. "But isn't it fun?" I offered him my finger. "If I tell you it's strawberry, you'll taste strawberry, I promise."

"I won't," he replied, but even then I didn't care. I told him a story about a friend I'd had for as long as I could remember. A girl just like me, who understood me in ways that nobody else did.

Sometimes she spent the night, a little shadow curled up with me under the blankets.

Around then I learned the best lies are half-truths. It was a lie that I had any friend for that long. It was a lie that anyone I knew would want to spend a whole night with me. But there was someone who slept with me, who lurked in my room at night. I didn't understand yet that it was me. My shadow self, being born as I invented new selves with the stories I told during the day.

Mr. Goodson nodded along like he believed that I wasn't lonely.

When I started junior high, I dreamt repeatedly of a woman I assumed was my mother. It was then that I finally began to believe she had existed. I thought of her as a winter woman, always appearing at a distance, walking along a snowy field. I finally saw a picture of her when I was twelve. The woman in the black-and-white square photograph leaned on a car, wearing denim and a loose floral shirt, sunglasses tucked between the top buttons. She looked nothing like the person in my dreams but rather like a photograph of my future self.

This is why I want to see a photograph of K, just to be sure that the girl in my dreams is really her. On Thursday afternoon, I trudge to the photography studio after class lets out, away from the stream of students heading toward the cafeteria for lunch. From the large lecture hall, I splash through the slushy drive, past colonial houses full of oddly-shaped classrooms. I cross paths only with the school's groundskeeper, whose face barely emerges from her hooded, cocoon-like coat. Though she doesn't bother to greet me, she watches me walk by with a steady gaze. My boots begin to take on water.

The arts building has a gridded face of windows, metal lines, and concrete. Unlike most of the undergraduate population, I am not an art student and don't know how to navigate its mazelike interior. All the studios look the same to me. I make several wrong turns, ask a group of liberally pierced upperclassmen where to go before I find my way. The photography professor is smoking out the window when I walk in. He flicks his cigarette into the snow and shuts it. The room takes on a brisk, ashy gust.

"Don't tell anyone," he says quickly. "It's too cold to be out there." The old man has a pockmarked face and plastic yellow glasses. His back curls forward a bit, and a coarse brush of gray stubble covers his face. "Can I help you?" he asks.

"I was wondering if you had some photographs by a former student." I weave between sagging couches, stacked flat-file drawers, and carts of well-worn photography books.

In one corner, an ominous black curtained doorway looms. I assume the darkroom lies beyond it. The curtain flutters for a moment, then stills.

"I have many," he says, gesturing to the flat files. "You'll have to be more specific."

"As far as I know, she was a photography major." I avoid eye contact, embarrassed.

"You must mean K." He steps away from the window. "You're not the first person to ask."

I hover as the photography professor shuffles to the flat files and taps a finger from drawer to drawer. In my head, I rehearse how to tell him I'm different from other curious undergrads. I have a relationship with the missing girl, or at least her ghost. I relish any chance to talk about K. She is the best story I have right now. In some ways, she feels like my only friend. As seconds stretch to minutes, I try to start the conversation. "Have you worked here long?"

"Too long," he says.

"Did you know K?"

He opens a flat file with no reply, the rusting metal scraping harshly. "She preferred medium format." He takes a large box out from the drawer and places it on the cutting table behind him. "Our Yashica TLR disappeared with her."

I open the box with breath held tight. I take the square photos out one by one. There are only eight. I recognize the campus in winter, though a few buildings are missing from its landscape. Some girls smoking outside the library with stares that decades later still say, *What are you looking at.* The empty picnic table under an old oak outside our dorm building, a dog-eared paperback on its bench. The view from what I've begun to think of as our room, mine and K's. It's completely unchanged—the same field and tree line I saw this morning, the greenhouse buried in snow, the groundskeeper's cabin with painted white siding and dark shutters. There are more uninteresting campus scenes. Only one image is less than perfect. It captures a woman in dark winter clothes and work boots sitting on a low stone wall. Part of the photograph is smoky, almost black, obscuring the woman's face.

"It wasn't fixed properly," the photography teacher says when I pause over it. "It's slowly turned from exposure to light."

"Oh," I say, not knowing what *fixed* means. A broken photograph? I point to the torso. "Is this her?"

He points to the hand resting on top of the wall beside her, his tobacco-stained fingertip almost touching mine. "That hand belongs to a much older person,"

I wonder for a moment whether I'm really looking for K or someone else. She may have walked away on her own, gotten lost or hurt with only herself to blame, but they never did find a body. If I assume she was taken, as most people do, another set of hands comes into play.

"Are there any photos of K?" I ask.

"None that I know of."

I put the photos carefully back and close the box. "Thank you."

He shrugs and turns his back to me, opening the flat file with that same tortured sound. A breeze whistles through the window. I walk past it on my way out. As I pull it closed tighter to seal any cracks, I see the groundskeeper approach her booth by the main drive. Just before she enters, she looks up, right at me. Even from this distance, her gaze beckons.

The groundskeeper spends part of every afternoon in the little shed by the main administrative building. From any angle, it looks like a tollbooth. Inside, she holds "office hours," in which students can come with any requests we might have. Mostly we come looking for lost items. Almost anything that disappears on campus winds up in that booth, our unofficial lost and found.

This is why, when I approach the window, she slides it open and asks, "What are you looking for?"

"K," I say, as though K is a friend I've lost in a crowd. The grounds-keeper studies me. She has violent eyes, crisp blue with pinhole pupils. A winter woman. I have a brief desire to crack her irises between my teeth like candy.

"What do you want to know?" she asks.

"Everything."

She sits back in her old gray office chair, her mouth sinking into her sweater's bulging cowl. Her right hand lingers on the sliding window, ready to snap it closed.

"I live in Lewis 309," I add, presenting this fact like a license to pry.

"Every year you girls come asking." She drops her hand into her lap. A blue vein streaks up from her wrist, forking elegantly at her knuckles.

"I see her every night in that room. I think she wants me to find out what happened to her."

"That's presumptuous." Her top lip emerges from the sweater like dawn. "Go on. I have work to do."

I step back, sinking into my scarf in a mirroring gesture. I keep my gaze on her for a few more paces, our eyes locked. I can be sharp too. My irises are so dark she'll never know where my pupils begin.

K

I spend the rest of the day combing through the library's measly collection of school records. They have nothing that predates 1995, when a fire tore through most of the library's collection. On my way out, I encounter Anya sitting on the floor between two study desks, several open books laid out around her and her laptop.

"Big test?" I ask.

"Paper," she says, barely glancing up.

"Hey, I was wondering . . ." I wait for her to stop typing, but she doesn't. "Do you know anything else about K?"

"What do you mean by 'else'?" Her fingers never pause.

"Like, more about her. Where did you hear about her?"

"My OL told me." She sighs. "I don't have time for your bullshit today."

I nod and begin to step away when she sighs again. "Listen. Nobody really knows anything. That's the whole mystery, right? She was just a student, and then one day she wasn't. Everything else is just made-up stories, which you would know all about."

That's never all there is. There's a truth, no matter how buried, no matter how many better, more appetizing truths have been spun around it. It's more obvious each day that I should have gone to a bigger school, where news of my bullshit wouldn't have spread so fast. I've run out of people who take me seriously, and I can't blame them for it.

I eat dinner, as always, in the last hour before the cafeteria gate rattles down between the tables and hot food. I prefer this time because I look less out of place surrounded by empty chairs.

Absorbed in the rhythmic clacking of my utensils, I begin to feel like I'm not really alone. K has never appeared to me outside our room—not yet. But there's another shadow: the me who gathered and grew in the corners of my bedroom at night long before I came here, long before I'd heard of K at all. At first I thought I would start fresh without her, leave her at home with my parents and old stuffed toys, but I realize now I can't. She grows stronger year by year, filled out by every lie I speak, every story that obscures my true story. I eat quickly, with determination, not wanting to see how defined she must be, what kind of face my words have carved into her shape.

The groundskeeper arrives when I'm halfway through my meal. She puts a little piece of everything onto her plate. She disappears from my sight for a few minutes, then emerges again to take a seat at the opposite end of the room, in the coldest corner, between two sets of wide windows. Her face looks ceramic, half in sodium light, half in fluorescent. She cuts up her food into small pieces but never brings her fork to her mouth, just like an anorexic girl I went to middle school with. Our eyes meet several times, too often to be coincidence. I know the groundskeeper has the answers I want, but we are at a stalemate. I can't tell if she's an enemy or an ally. As someone who wields words recklessly, I find her silence infuriating. Despite this, I love being looked at.

On Friday night I sit outside a party with a group of seniors who don't know me. I bum a cigarette and tell them between drags that, really, K haunts my room. By tomorrow they too will believe it's a lie, but in this moment they stare in drunken rapture as I hold court in the corner of the porch, an elbow on each railing.

"I think we have a connection. Sometimes I feel like I am her, she is me. Think about it. My name is Kara with a *K*." I bring my drink to my lips, raising my eyebrows for effect.

"Have you ever tried a séance?" the girl who gave me the cigarette asks.

"That shit is fake," I reply, not wanting to admit that I'm afraid. I let them follow me home. Three girls: Lora, Yuko, and Marcy, tall and spindly with big, crunching boots.

It's past midnight. I expect K to be waiting when I walk in, but the room is empty.

Lora has candles in her backpack, and I don't ask why. Yuko tapes a plastic bag around the smoke detector. Marcy takes out the old Zippo she used on our cigarettes and lights the candles in a ring around us. I expect them to do something corny, call out to the spirits and such, but instead the three girls form a circle around me and lie on the ground. They buck their hips toward the ceiling, toward me, toward the ceiling again. Yuko begins to hum a discordant note, and Marcy whispers something furtive to the tiled floor. She licks the dirt that trails from my shoes each night. They hold each other's ankles. They suck each other's toes. Their bodies become shapeless in the candlelight, white streaks emerging from their dark clothing, disappearing into each other's mouths. The three bodies turn into one shape, and the smell of wax melting brings me back to a storm six years ago that took the power from our building. I was alone with a lit candle. The whole apartment had turned into a gaping mouth, the wax its saliva pooling on the dining table.

Who was I that night, without my father's voice in the living room, my stepmother's bare feet on the carpet? No classmates, no neighbors on our dark, breathless street. For hours, someone sat before me at the dining table. I couldn't see her face beyond the murmur of a single candle flame, but I knew it was my shadow self.

In my dorm room, she steps out of my skin and circles the writhing girls in wait. Her silhouette looks just like K. She pushes me to the ground, and I close my eyes before I can see her face. She leans down and sucks my neck. I shiver. She dares me to want and I do, I do, I want something, but I don't know if it's her or K or the truth or something else entirely. I wait for her teeth, but they never come.

When I open my eyes, it's morning. The girls are gone, and the candles have burned into puddles of wax. The ceiling hatch is open, the lock lying on the ground not far from me, the mess of piping within exposed. It stares at me like an open eye.

What I've never told anyone: Just once, I forgot my lunch in my cubby, and Mr. Goodson accompanied me to retrieve it. In the empty hallway, as I fished around in my backpack, he stood a little too close, leaning against the cubby beside mine. He took my free hand and licked every finger silently while I whispered flavors: strawberry, cherry, blueberry, grape, watermelon. It was exactly what I had wanted, and yet I didn't feel satisfied—only ashamed. When he was done, he licked his lips with closed eyes, savoring the fruit-salad taste. I took my lunch box, and we never spoke of my fingers again.

Standing on a chair, I reach carefully into the open hatch. I fish out two items tucked into the crawl space. One is a boxlike camera with two lenses. The top flap opens like origami to reveal a large viewfinder. The metal script above the top lens reads *Yashica*. I have no idea how to use it, so I set it on the empty desk. The other is a metal tea tin printed with oranges. Strips of developed film lie curled inside. I hold the inverted images to the light. Some are more dull campus scenes, but many feature a naked woman with long hair and blunt fringe. Both her hair and skin must be light because they're nearly black on the negative. Among the strips I find a folded piece of yellowing paper. It's lined and has one frayed side, clearly torn from a notebook. In black ink, it reads:

> I fell in love with the groundskeeper the moment I saw her. I don't know if love is even the right word. It's like that moment maybe a few pages or maybe just a few sentences into a book when you realize, *I never want to put this down.* You stay awake all night reading it. You forget to eat. Your life halts until it's complete. This is what happened when she opened the cabin door.

I recall the first night K appeared on the opposite bed. I don't know if it was love either, but it's true that I couldn't look away. I savored our nights beside each other, forgetting that K could never be mine. Something took her. Through my window, the groundskeeper's cabin stares across the field. I pull down the shade violently, but it trembles and flies back up, refusing to close. I read the note out loud, trying to imagine what it would sound like in K's voice.

I want to find the three girls to return Marcy's lighter and learn more about last night's ritual. I ask around groups of seniors in the dining hall, but nobody knows who I'm talking about. Once breakfast ends and the cafeteria empties, I go to the groundskeeper's booth. Behind the glass, she looks hesitant to crack the window. Finally, she opens a slit. "Can I help you?"

I slip Marcy's Zippo through the slim gap. "This was lost." The groundskeeper takes the silver lighter between two long, chapped fingers.

"Where did you get it?" she asks.

"A senior named Marcy."

The groundskeeper pockets it, squinting her eyes to knife blades.

"This too," I say, pulling the camera from my bag, hoping it will convince her to tell me what she knows.

She opens the window wider and takes the camera. She stares at its lenses, eye to eye.

"It was in my room. I think it belongs to the school."

She sets it down. "You should have just taken it to the photography department."

"I wanted to bring it to you."

K

Our groundskeeper has a blunt fringe and light hair too, though it's cropped at her chin. A sharp shadow connects her cheekbone to her jaw. She has thin pink lips. I want to fall in love with her like K did, but it's difficult. Even though I think she's beautiful in a brutal way, nothing inside me stirs. Still, I have to try.

She leans through the window, her face flushing as it meets the cold air. "What else are you looking for?"

"The truth," I say. She lifts her eyebrows like she wants to laugh. I step back. "Or whatever you know."

"Just remember this: she's not your friend." The groundskeeper shuts the window. She doesn't understand. K and I are more than friends. We're the same.

"I love her, I love her, I love her," I whisper like a spell as I walk away. I want to understand how K's groundskeeper moved her even though my groundskeeper has spiderlike hands that make my body seize up and prepare for flight. I think about the way all my muscles pulled tight when Mr. Goodson took my fingers into his mouth. Maybe this too is love.

Later in my room, I kneel on my bed and press the negatives against the window. There's one image that doesn't fit with the rest. A woman against a car. A floral shirt, a pair of sunglasses. I squint, but I can't make out her face.

The empty bed creaks behind me. I keep still, my palm turning cold against the glass. I've never seen K in daylight. I'm afraid she won't look anything like the girl in my dreams. I still don't know what happened to K, whether she was left whole or mangled inside out.

She joins me on the bed. She doesn't smell like death or girl but like a wet dog, fresh from an autumn night. Her arm reaches past me. It is identical to mine. K taps the window glass with her fingertip. I adjust my focus from her nail to the scene beyond: the groundskeeper's porch light, yellow even as the day turns blue. K pulls back her hand.

I turn, expecting a mirror—my own shadow given flesh—but there's nothing. Something flits through the opening in the ceiling, but it could be an insect or a mouse, and then it's gone.

I cross the darkening field to the groundskeeper's cabin. The door opens before I can knock. "I thought you'd be stupid enough to come." She steps aside so I can enter. Only the kitchen light is on. I close the door behind me and follow her in, leaving a wet trail.

"Nobody cared about that girl until she was gone." The groundskeeper sits at the table, and I sit across from her. "Now you come knocking."

"I just want to know what happened to her, why she haunts my room."

"Is that all?" The groundskeeper's teeth catch the kitchen light, her lips stretching around a perfect mouth.

"I love you," I say. "I fell in love with you the moment I saw you. I don't know if love is the right word."

"Enough." She reaches across the table and covers my mouth with her hand. "Be careful with words that aren't yours." With her free hand, she points to the corner behind my right shoulder. I turn my head slightly, though her hand remains clamped on my mouth. Through the corner of my eye, I see the shadow I call K lurking in the gap between the stove and the wall.

"You've been feeding her all this time, making her bigger and hungrier. Do you even know who she is?" the groundskeeper asks.

"K," I try to say, but I can't open my mouth to form the syllable. I bite one of the groundskeeper's fingers, and a piece of her skin sloughs off into my mouth like it's wrapping paper. I gag, wanting desperately to spit it out, but I can't wriggle out of her grasp. I have no choice; I swallow it. The wound is slippery against my lips and tastes sour.

"You don't even know K." The groundskeeper laughs, and I count too many teeth. "Since you've come this far, I'll tell you."

K's last winter here was in 1985, when our school was still a women's college. A blizzard was due any day, and the Lewis dorm, mostly unchanged since that afternoon, was a flurry of puffy coats and stomping boots, suitcases pulled through hallways. K, who was freshly orphaned and had no home to go to, had requested to remain in the dorms for the monthlong winter break. The school, taking pity on her, allowed it. They told her the groundskeeper would be around and could take her into town if she needed anything. As long as she was comfortable using the dorm kitchen, there would be no problem.

While the other students piled into their parents' cars or dragged their suitcases to the airport shuttle, K sat on the picnic table outside the dorm in her winter coat and gingham slippers. She puffed a cigarette and watched her classmates evacuate through the crosshatched screen of the borrowed Yashica TLR. It was her favorite camera—she had checked it out from the photography department months earlier and refused to return it. Her classmates had resigned themselves to letting her have it. Most preferred the Hasselblad for medium format anyway.

One by one the cars departed. The airport-goers gathered by the campus center, piled into a school bus, and disappeared down the drive. By midafternoon, K was entirely alone. Nineteen and not much of a chef, she had stockpiled Campbell's cans on the last shuttle trip into town. She was about to tackle one with a can opener when a phone rang.

Back then, Lewis had a row of three phone booths in the hallway beneath the main staircase—what is now a closet. K approached the middle booth hesitantly. The last time she had been in one of these phone booths, a man told her through the receiver that her grandmother had passed unexpectedly in her sleep. What he didn't say, but she knew nonetheless: *You are alone now.*

K picked up the receiver and spoke a quiet hello. She assumed it was a parent searching for a student who had already departed, but an unfamiliar voice said, "You're home, then."

"Who is this?"

"Are you going to make soup by yourself?" the voice continued. K liked its sound and tried to imagine the neck it sprang from.

"Maybe," she replied, not knowing what else to say.

"Come to my place before the storm gets too bad. I'm making stew."

"Where? I still don't know who this is."

The voice laughed. "Who do you think? There's only the two of us left on campus."

K hung up the receiver and put away the unopened can. It was still early in the day, but the coming blizzard cupped the landscape in eerie shadow. She put on her boots and coat. The Yashica bounced against her stomach as she strode across the dry brown field toward the greenhouse. Nestled in its side was the only other light on campus.

"This," I interrupt, the word a muffled syllable behind the grounds-keeper's hand. She releases my mouth, and I say clearly, "This is the moment."

"What moment?" The groundskeeper peels the skin off her hand like a glove, flexing the dark talons that emerge. The shadow in the corner edges closer, waiting for my next words. She is K, but she's also something more that has known me for years and years. The air behind me turns warm with her anticipation.

"She opened the cabin door," I say, not wanting to let the shadow and the groundskeeper hear K's words through my mouth again.

K's thoughts then don't need to be repeated. The groundskeeper looked down with glacial eyes, and K knew that she would not be alone again. She never returned to the dorm. Night after night, she remained in the groundskeeper's house even though she was never asked to stay. She cut herbs from the hothouse for dinner. She swept the floors while the groundskeeper left in her big-wheeled truck to buy groceries in town. For the first few days, K slept politely on the couch, listening to the groundskeeper pace in the room above. One night K followed her upstairs with the fluffiest couch cushion. A nest took up most of the bedroom, filled with pelts and hide. K climbed in, and when the groundskeeper didn't tell her to leave, she slept in its animal smell.

"Did you love K?" I ask when the groundskeeper has finished removing the human mask from her snout and pulled the blond hair off like a hood. I'm certain that, like K, I will never leave this cabin.

"Does it matter?" the groundskeeper replies.

It didn't matter to K. In the morning she woke, pulled herself from the cocoon of pelts, and reached for her camera. She balanced on the edge of the nest and took photographs of the groundskeeper's naked body while she slept, her smooth limbs amphibian against all that fur. Later, after the film had run out, K took the groundskeeper's heavy key ring in the middle of the night and tried each one of the doors to the darkroom until she was inside. In the red light, K watched that same body take shape in the chemical bath like an embryo growing in the womb. Inverted, it was black and insect-like.

When K returned at dawn, another storm kept the sunlight at bay. She took off her clothes in the wan morning. She climbed on top of the groundskeeper and pressed their bodies together. The groundskeeper opened her eyes and finally asked, "You like this skin, don't you?"

K pressed overgrown fingernails into the groundskeeper's stomach. "Yes. Very much."

The older woman seemed to notice her for the first time, a ripe fruit growing on a barren plant. She had become used to the sound of the girl's breath buried near her own.

She turned K onto her back and kneeled before her. "Do you want to stay?"

K nodded.

Using one long fingernail, the creature split a seam from her own chin down to her clitoris and opened herself like a winter coat. K crawled inside that warm, wet womb and remained, unborn in the body she loved so much.

"How could I say no?" The beast, now fully undressed before me, holds my hand between two of hers. "It's what she wanted. She was the only one so willing until you."

"Is that the truth?" I ask.

"Of course." Her voice is sweet, her eyes still marble blue. "Is there a better truth?"

The shadow places its hands on my shoulders, waiting for me to give in. I do. Easily. "There's always a better truth," I say.

The beast raises my hand to her mouth, licks it, and says, "Tell us. We're so hungry."

"We are the same, K and I."

The shadow takes a bite out of my shoulder. It's a new kind of pain.

"K had no mother."

The beast sinks her teeth into my wrist. I whine as she snaps the tendons that reach all the way to my fingers, but I don't pull away. This is what I wanted, perhaps what I've always wanted.

"She was never born," I continue.

The shadow tilts my chin back and chews up my neck. "And she never died."

The beast, impatient, claws at my forearm to bring me toward her. The shadow yanks back, not wanting to let go. They draw closer to each other, my body the tether between them.

"She only disappeared."

The words come out of me like a sigh. They rip up more flesh, lap up the blood that spills out, take me apart on the table with their mouths. I love the texture of their tongues on my bones. They save my face for last so I can keep telling this story, until all our lips come together in a kiss.

In the Winter

I become quite pretty in the winter, in those dim afternoons with sheet-metal skies. I line my lips with brown, burgundy, and wine and whiskey stains. I crave bright fruits as though they'll substitute the daylight—sunset persimmons, sunrise grapefruit, late afternoon mandarins crushed into the horizon bisecting my dark mouth. This is why he noticed me between the bare trees.

Where are you going, class is starting soon. That was none of his business, but he asked anyway, just to talk to me, I think.

The cemetery, I replied, because I thought that would make me seem interesting somehow, to be caught eating a clementine on a gravestone.

You've already missed one, he said. So he had noticed me, slipping in and out of the lecture hall seat closest to the door.

I don't have the book, I said. (I did; it was in my bag.) It will be pointless for me to go.

Come and listen.

No.

I walked away, satisfied to know his gaze had not been an accident. He liked to sit by me, close enough to catch my tangy scent of what was once citrus, now turned sour from spit and the oil in my hair. Did he like that smell?

He didn't follow me, and I never went to the graveyard. I went home and ate soup alone at the wooden dining table between the damask wallpaper. I hate to eat hot things, too-wet too-solid things, in front of other people. I don't like to show my teeth or risk a small drip from my lips. I drop silverware a lot. Was I lonely back then? Of course I was. Who wasn't lonely "back then." In the winter I'm pretty because the loneliness makes my face slack, my eyes intense. There are no stories without loneliness.

He sat beside me in the cafeteria, where I was alone with a sketchbook and some fruit and the plastic container I would fill with things to eat when I was home later. I knew other people coveted his company, but he chose me. Maybe because I looked pathetic, or maybe because he liked to watch my fingernails dig and carve into pith.

I have the book if you want it. I've read it many times already if you want to borrow it.

What makes you think I'll read it.

You'll have to write about it eventually.

I don't have to do anything. (But I did.)

Here was the plan. I would go to his place to pick up the book. He could have handed it over in a hallway or across a cafeteria table, but instead he chose to invite me to retrieve it, so I knew there was more to it. Especially at that age, when we all sought excuses to make more of things. It was a warm afternoon for that time of year, so when the sky shed it was wet and unpretty. His room smelled kind of like weed, but a lit candle cast cypress and cloves over it. A little redundant in these months when only the evergreens have sound or smell. He handed me the book and I examined the cover, its neutrals and black serif title.

What's it about?

Two women who are friends but also not friends.

I lay on his bed without invitation, on my stomach, with my shins dangling off, the book open in front of me. His duvet smelled deep-in-closet musty, like maybe he hadn't washed it since last winter. I waited for his voice, or perhaps the creak or sag of the bed under his weight, but instead I felt a hand, warm and large, on the back of my neck. I waited to be yanked up or pressed in, but neither happened.

Don't hate me for this, he said. I don't do this with anyone.

Read? I asked, turning my head so my cheek rested on paper. He didn't acknowledge my weak joke. I closed my eyes and felt his fingers, the other ones.

It was a strange way to come—tights pulled only to my knees, treated a bit like a fleshy little vegetable that had to be held down and scraped clean of seeds—but it worked. Sometimes sex isn't sexy, just effective. I left a dark spit mark on a block of dialogue in his book. I tried to turn around, offer something inevitably awkward in thanks or return, but his hand tightened on my neck—Stay there. Don't look at me.

How many orgasms does it take to achieve intimacy? How many times does a thing fuck you from behind before you realize you only ever saw him in the woods, in the cafeteria with meat between his teeth. In that classroom, where you were both supposed to be the closest to human, with his hair combed smooth, coat buttoned, scarf tight, he looked completely different. Maybe not even the same thing that fucked you from behind over and over and never let you see his eyes when he came because they were violet, gold, cut with oblong pupils. Sometimes you glimpse his hand on the bed beside you, and the hairs on his knuckles look thicker than you remember, and you realize your own hand underneath is small, soft, sticky-spitty like a toddler's.

Was I the creature, or was he? Because the walls changed, I know they did. The doors disappeared. Outside became black not with night but because we took the room and tipped it into another world where it was never supposed to be, left a double of it behind so nobody would know. The magic came from somewhere, but with our bodies so tightly pressed it was hard to say where.

How did I escape that room, you ask, and I'll tell you that to out-grow a room is not to leave it, only swallow hard and walk around with it rattling inside you until eventually you fill up with enough things that it doesn't make a sound.

Anomaly

I downloaded a dating app for the first time in two years on an ordinary Wednesday for no reason except that the sun was out in full force, turning the concrete outside the office window white as linen. It was a nice day to go on a date, to drink outside on a bustling patio. The last date I'd been on was in college. He had been an older man, twenty-seven or so, I think, who bought me dinner now and again and, if I was in the mood, took me home for the night. Good enough company to talk to about TV and movies and complain about mundane things. That's all I'd wanted in those days, still only a year or so after Olivia and I ended things.

I wasn't sure what I wanted this time, but it was comforting to swipe on face after face, knowing there were this many people who were also alone, also looking for something. It had been some time since anyone felt comfortable meeting strangers, not while the time war was still ongoing in some distant future.

Until the armistice a year ago, the news cycle had reminded us every day to be wary of new faces: *Be careful who you talk to, what questions you answer, what favors you agree to.* Highly trained time agents with conflicting political agendas waged a silent war on our streets over issues we hadn't even conceived of yet. Envoys from the future, who we'd come to know as temporal diplomats, informed us that these were the crucial years, when our timelines made contact for the first time, and the human world surged with new possibilities. Every decision being made by our best scientists, most active social movements, and influential world leaders would shape everything, though we weren't told how. After a while, they said that even conversation was risky, that any encounter could set in motion unforeseeable changes to our timeline that may or may not be welcome. We all downloaded apps that used various profiles to map how many degrees of acquaintance we had with others in a room. People with no connections came up on the screen as bright red dots. Paranoia kept doors locked, blinds drawn. When the temporal diplomats announced the truce, we had no way to verify their claims but wanted to believe it was over because we were lonely.

My timer went off just as I got my first match, and I trudged back to my desk for the second half of my shift. My company had taken the year before armistice to do extensive renovations, reasoning that keeping most of the employees at home would reduce risk of time-line alteration. The new digs were shiny and full of perks like an espresso machine and smoothie stations bursting with fresh fruit to lull us into corporate-culture hypnosis. But these renovations were hard to fall for in the customer service department, which had gone from largely forgotten to a horrible kind of surveillance state. Our cubicles were replaced by soundproof booths with transparent walls. We were each given a cup of dry-erase markers to take notes on the glass like it was a fun, cool thing, but every inch of our workspace was now visible to the managers, who paced the aisles between meetings like wardens. Unable to pull out our phones or swipe onto an online shopping tab when we were ahead on our numbers, support agents made existential eye contact with one another during phone calls. We tried to pass time between tickets with clandestine games of hangman on the sections of the glass wall by our knees. It was surreal to spend the workday watching mouths move all around but only hear my own voice appeasing unhappy customers.

I ran into Jenni, who worked in the booth beside mine, at the mouth of our aisle. We exchanged haggard looks. Lately the queue had been consistently over 1K because of the postarmistice surge of users on our coupon-clipping app.

She paused. "We have four minutes still."

I turned my phone screen toward her. "I'm back on the apps."

"Okay, fun. Everyone's getting back out there these days. Big pool!" Jenni always said vague things about dating because she recently married her college sweetheart after an eight-year relationship and was amnesic about what it was like to be single. I liked her for this because she was happy in such an uncomplicated way. She never wanted to trade relationship woes, and so our conversations never led to Olivia.

"We can look more in the cave." That's what Jenni and I called this alcove we had managed to make by positioning our rolling drawer sets mirrored just so to give us a little shelter to check our phones.

As soon as I signed into my phone shift, I got a call from a woman asking about her pastry BOGO.

"I was planning on bringing the second one home for my son. Can you imagine the tantrum when we had to split the chocolate croissant in the end?"

I spent five minutes explaining that croissants were not in fact part of the BOGO deal before slapping her with remediation credit and ending the call.

My phone pinged, and I pulled it out in the cave.

Hey what would you say are your top three physical features?

I started typing something about cheekbones and thick hair but then realized this was stupid and I was mostly just describing Olivia. I pocketed my phone.

I answered a few emails and then got pinged by a beautiful girl with dark curls: *Wanna start a summer fling?*

Did I? I didn't respond because truly I wasn't sure.

By the time my next call ended, I had another message from a guy named Charlie: *Has anyone ever told you that you look really cute in a sari*

I blocked him.

A ping from José, who I recognized from some other department in our company: *How many dates would it take you to break my heart?*

Cringey, but it made me realize my profile was the same as when I was about to move after college: *looking for something casual and fun before changing cities.* I hadn't even glanced at it since then because the thought of having to craft something newly punchy and cute stressed me out. But an office romance did sound kind of interesting. Our workplace already gave us common ground, though I had only encountered him once or twice in the café and clearly left no impression.

Guess you'll have to find out, I replied.

A few minutes later, José responded: *I hope we can make it through at least 4.*

I tucked my phone away as a group of managers spilled out of the conference room for a bathroom break. The department leaderboard had me smack-dab in the middle yet again but meeting my numbers all the same. I worked slowly through a long troubleshooting email before sliding my phone out in the cave and asking José, *What's your plan for the first 3?*

He typed for a while before sending *Coffee museum drink with an epic sweeping romance in between. Then heartbreak.*

I closed the app in mild disgust. You would think the introduction of time travel and extratemporal diplomats and stealthy timeline-disrupting agents would give everyone a new perspective on life. Our species was allegedly on the cusp of evolution, spies sweeping in from the future to influence us, but people were still as corny and boring as ever.

By the end of my early shift, we hit the midweekday lull. Calls slowed while people got busy with the homestretch of their workdays, picking up kids and whatnot. Jenni and I spent some time swiping, her giving subtle thumbs-ups and -downs as we shot glances at the screen.

In the last hour of work, I received a message from a guy named Amir, who had been good-enough looking, albeit not particularly remarkable aside from the fact that he looked maybe Desi (common ground, hopefully).

It's a beautiful day. We matched. Should we just fuck it and go on a date tonight?

Why not? I replied. *What do you want to do?*

We could do the usual thing—drinks, dinner

Somehow I think there's an or

Haha OR, randomly, I have tickets to the anomaly

I looked up to see if Jenni was reading the message, but she had her eyes on her screen, mouth moving soundlessly as she clicked around.

The anomalies were these little shimmery tears that opened all over the world when too many particles whipped through time at once. The time war supposedly ended to prevent more from popping up. They were unpredictable and frightening, with the potential to shred the fabric of time and space. You walked into some and emerged from others. Some you walked into and didn't come out at all—at least not in this time, this universe. Most were under lock and key, tightly secured and surveilled by their country's border patrol, but the ones with entry and exit points close together were quickly monetized by their governments. Within months of determining that walking through an anomaly was mostly harmless—like going through a tunnel—as long as you went with a buddy, governments established protocols and booking systems and exorbitant fees.

Predictably, humanity couldn't invent anything without fucking up the environment and commodifying what was left. The anomaly in Illinois, about forty-five minutes from my city, had two ends in neighboring cornfields. The necessity of traversing in pairs made it a coveted date spot, equipped with a mini train that drove from one end to another and stands that sold locally made pies, cider, and fried cheese curds. Tickets needed to be purchased months in advance. I had already seen a flurry of frightening engagement photos taken in the tall grass in front of the shiny little gash, a newly adorned ring finger glinting in the anomaly's strange light. There was something off about people who were fresh out, a harrowed look in their eyes that evoked certain types of addicts or insomniacs, yet the captions to the photos were jarringly bland: *My best friend and I decided to take the leap after walking through time together. Truly one of the most beautiful experiences of my life. I love you so much, Scott.* Clearly not a first-date kind of thing.

That doesn't sound random, I replied when it became clear Jenni was wrapped up in a long call.

Ok, I got them a long time ago, but my plans fell through.

Isn't this kind of psycho for a first date?

I thought it might be a fun experiment. If we hate it, we'll never have to talk to each other again.

My shift ended, and I waited for Jenni to finish up her call. She groaned as she stepped out. "Who says 'pastry' but doesn't include croissants?"

We fell into step as we emerged in the hallway, swinging into the bathroom on our way to the elevator—a postshift ritual where we traded complaints while Jenni reapplied whatever bright lipstick she was sporting that day.

I leaned against the tiled wall and listened to her rant about the BOGO deal until I had the opportunity for an extreme non sequitur. "You and Jason did the anomaly, right?"

Jenni unscrewed her lipstick. "Yeah, why?"

"What's it like? Everyone makes such a big deal."

Jenni paused, applicator wand raised halfway to her mouth. "It's hard to describe. Weird, like a shared dream. It was, like, fine— definitely overhyped. We didn't feel 'connected' or 'changed' afterward. I think you might trade some atoms or electrons or something with the person who goes with you, but Jason says that sort of exchange is pretty much meaningless scientifically, unless you give it spiritual significance."

I considered this. Jenni and Jason seemed completely normal. They went through the anomaly and still had a barnyard wedding and meal prepped on Sundays, and here she was complaining about croissants. I showed her Amir's messages.

"I mean, why not? Pretty low-risk. Tons of people, high security. When else will you go?"

"Is it worth it?"

Jenni dropped her lipstick into her bag and gave her reflection a long look, gaze fixed on her own eyes. "I don't know if I can answer that for you."

Amir and I met an hour before his ticket time so we could get acquainted over a beer at one of the food stands by the anomaly. He arrived in a T-shirt and jeans and was of average physique, slightly shorter than his photos made him seem (of course). We sat at a picnic table with overpriced lagers. It was just past seven, but in late June, the sky was still blue. I learned that Amir was an engineer at a power-tool company. I shruggingly told him I worked customer service.

"That sounds nice, talking to people all day." He picked at the label on his bottle. "It gets lonely in the lab sometimes."

"I guess, but it makes me not want to talk to people after work."

"Like me?" He smiled, teasing.

I smiled back. "Yeah, I hate this."

I was trying my best to be flirty, and I think he was too, but something wasn't clicking. Maybe it was just as I had said: I spent all day talking to people, and here I was making small talk with another stranger. I had forgotten how much I disliked these ice-breaking conversations. I had nothing interesting to say about myself. My life was simple: I went to work, picked up groceries on the way home, made dinner, ate in front of the TV. In the summer, I took bike rides or bought flowers at the farmers market. Read a novel on the weekend. Most of my friends lived out of state, so my social scene was contained to seeing my sister and her family every couple weeks, watching a movie with my roommates occasionally, and grabbing a drink with Jenni once in a blue moon. I didn't mind, though. There were many think pieces written about what it meant to socialize when you were so afraid of anyone you didn't know. Personally, I was more comfortable on my own, with no need to worry about how other people perceived me. Even when it became safe to mingle again, I continued my reclusive lifestyle. Sure, if I really psychoanalyzed myself, I could connect my recent affinity for detachment to my breakup with Olivia somehow, but what did it matter? I was allowed to be happy regardless.

I took a swig of my beer. "We're about to go into the anomaly together, so let's skip the pleasantries."

Amir turned his bottle and started on the opposite corner of the label. "Okay."

"Who did you originally plan on bringing here?"

Amir laughed. "An ex, obviously."

"I knew it," I replied.

"My turn," Amir said. "What happened with your most recent ex?"

"She died."

Amir's smile fell for a moment, and his eyes changed into this big, shiny, apologetic look. It was comical how sudden and typical his reaction was.

"Just kidding." I smirked.

He sighed, then laughed again. "That is *not* funny. I was panicking."

"My ex broke up with me a few years ago. Haven't talked to her since. Uncomplicated stuff."

Kind of. Olivia was diagnosed with late-stage cancer halfway through college, after we'd been together for a year. It was the strangest experience I ever had, a cinematic melodrama brought to life. I can't remember if I cried much or processed the unexpected weight of it. Instead I railed uppers and made the three-hour drive to her hometown every weekend to visit her, taking advantage of the time we had before she had to prep for surgery. One Sunday, as we lay in bed saying our goodbyes before I drove back, Olivia said, "I think it's time for us to break up."

I stopped grinding my teeth to listen. "What do you mean?"

She held me closer, rubbing my arm with her hand. "I love you, and I've loved our time together, but I really just want to be with my family right now. And I think you should spend more time at school."

I hadn't considered before then that I may have been intruding. It's true we had only been together a year, but it was also true that it had been an incredible year, and I had never felt so close to anyone in my life. First love was always life-or-death like that, at least until things became literally life-or-death. Olivia, already in her pajamas, walked me outside and waited at the doorway while I drove off. She looked thin and tired against the tall doorframe but so beautiful with her head leaning into the heavy evening colors, disappearing behind a bare hydrangea bush. We lost touch quickly after that. Some years later, her mother called to let me know Olivia hadn't made it. I took some days off and booked a hotel room for her funeral, but I couldn't go in the end. I wanted to be left with that girl who waved me into the night, because that's how she chose to leave me.

There was a huge amount of protests about the fact that the temporal diplomats would share none of their future technology and medical advancements with us. Their only goal was to regain control of the guerrilla time agents. The past was not to be otherwise tampered with. While this debate dominated the news, classmates I knew tangentially in college contacted me out of the blue to ask how I was feeling, given what happened to Olivia. Already I could sense what would create this future war—people blindly rejecting the inevitable, unchangeable nature of our reality. But I had already accepted that Olivia was gone irreversibly, and in my remaining years of college I learned that solitude suited me.

"Why did you want to see the anomaly?" I asked Amir, trying to change the subject.

He shrugged. "Honestly, I didn't. I think it's kind of weird. To stretch out your molecules like that? The fact that if you go in alone, you might not come back the same? Freaky. But my ex really wanted to go. I thought about just giving her the tickets after she broke up with me, but then decided to keep them out of spite."

I smiled. I always respected a spite move.

"What about you?" he asked.

I looked at the couples queuing up before their time slots, already hand in hand. They all looked like suckers, waiting to plunge into something unearthly just to slap clichés over it afterward. "I think I just want to know."

"What do you think is in there?"

"I heard it was like a dream, but nobody ever says anything that's not vague."

"Yeah. Everyone I know talks about it differently." Amir reached across the table and touched my left fingertips with his right ones. "We don't know anything about each other. Do you think that will matter?"

We could have looked up some articles about people who went into the anomaly with strangers, but at this point, that would have felt like cheating. I shrugged and slid the pad of my middle finger gently over his fingernail, pressing down on its unfamiliar shape.

"I want to know too," Amir said. "It sounds nice—dreaming with someone else." Amir and I locked eyes then, the closest to intimate we'd gotten. His expression had the hopeful desperation of a dog at the front door, waiting for someone to let him out into the bright world. Despite acting casual, he wanted connection as badly as any other lame person on the app. And maybe I was one of those lame people too, even if I felt myself going numb at the thought. I smiled with as much enthusiasm as I could muster. "Let's do it."

ANOMALY GUIDELINES

- Do not enter the anomaly alone. The person alongside you will be your body's blueprint for reentering reality. Staying hand in hand guarantees that your composition remains unchanged despite any distortions your molecules experience while traveling through the anomaly.

- The path is not visible, but you will be able to sense it. Do not stray, or you will risk getting lost between anomalies. We can only guarantee your safety if you stay on the path, and we will not be liable for wanderers.

- Do not be alarmed by the other presence you pass on your journey. Feelings of fear and anxiety are natural during this encounter, but they will pass. Stay focused on your companion and the path ahead. The entity is an ever-present but harmless observer.

- It's normal to feel dizziness or nausea after emerging. Take a moment to lie in the grass and rest as you reintegrate.

- Please support our local businesses! We're grateful to the community for hosting this experience for all of us to enjoy.

- Trains between anomalies run every half hour. See the host on the other side for directions to the pickup location.

Amir and I, exchanging glances, signed the waiver that came with the guidelines. It was a lot less straightforward than I had expected, and I could tell he thought the same. We passed the tablet to the couple behind us. I felt a prick of anxiety then, fully realizing I was to enter this uncertain space alongside someone I hardly knew. What if he went rogue somewhere in between, let go of my hand, or led me off the path? But Amir looked equally nervous, and I had a feeling that he was trustworthy, however misplaced that feeling may have been. Was I trustworthy? I could see Amir pondering this in the searching way he watched me. We were now only two couples from the front. He offered me his hand, and I took it. It was much larger than mine. I liked how new his fingers felt, their shape invoking no memories or emotion. Whatever the experience, it would be fresh. The sun was getting lower now, and the fields around us began taking on that nice deep yellow. Golden hour. Amir and I too were turning a rich honeyed color. The late evening became us. Through any lens, it was romantic.

I wondered how it would feel to be stretched like putty. What kind of dream would our molecules blend into? How would I be put back together in relation to Amir's body? I stared at my own calves and thighs, the floral tattoo above my knee, the pudgy little toes coming out of my sandals. Fine hair like shreds of gold leaf along my arm. I was beautiful, yet I couldn't think of a single piece of me worth salvaging from the pull of the universe.

It was about to be our turn now. The host in the black polo and cargo shorts droned a reiteration of the guidelines. I looked at Amir, and he looked at me with a nervous smile, and suddenly all of this felt dumb. We were suckers too, and the worst kinds—risking it all on a stranger just to feel close to someone. What could our shared dream show us? A numbness overtook any tenderness I had felt at the picnic table. The shimmer looked less special now that the Earth had reached its most picturesque slice of day; the anomaly was just another gleaming thing in a glut of light. No more breathtaking than a curtain in the wind. I let go of Amir's hand and stepped in alone, the protests from him and the host dissipating as quickly as my stupid little toes crossed into the opening.

For a moment, I was free-falling, not fast but a kind of Alice-drifting-down-the-rabbit-hole fall. I squeezed my eyes shut. My stomach heaved like I was careening down the tallest hump of a roller coaster. I felt that nervous lurch through my whole body, like my muscles and skin were getting displaced by inertia alongside my organs. I landed, sort of. Rather than my feet touching anything solid, I simply stopped moving eventually and leveled off. I sensed an immediate tug from the base of my throat that didn't move me—only beckoned. The path, I assumed. I opened my eyes.

I had expected something akin to the photographs of space in textbooks and on NASA's website, but everything was just black. I walked forward, unsure of what to do, afraid that coming alone had only ruined the experience. To my relief, a dim world came into view. Grass and dirt bloomed around my toes, yellow birch trees near my shoulders. A hike Olivia and I had taken on a trip to

Colorado the weekend of her cousin's wedding, right before she got sick. I had horrible altitude sickness that day but still managed to feel some awe in the terrain's novelty, having spent my life in Midwest flatlands. I was content to follow Olivia's shoulders emerging sweat-shined from a lavender racerback.

Here, though, I was alone. Despite the incline of the hike, I could feel that I was still walking on the path.

A horrible sensation crept up on me. Something was behind me, not far. I felt rather than heard its approach. Goose bumps stippled my skin. It was how I imagined a rabbit felt when a human, so capable of hurting it in so many ways, encountered it on a quiet street once thought to be empty. The entity, I assumed, narrowed the space behind us with each step. I thought it would cross my path, not follow me like it was hunting. I tried my best to walk straight on as the guidelines stated, but I had no distractions, no companion. It got closer. The beauty of the scene trembled under the weight of my fear. I imagined gruesome things—sharp teeth, wild eyes—abstract nightmares my brain sometimes conjured at night. I felt the entity's breath, not the hot breath of an animal, maybe not breath at all, but the pulsing of something alive and very close.

"You came alone." Olivia's voice, close to my ear.

I stopped walking, angry that it chose her of all people. "What do you want?" My mouth moved, but something not quite a sound came out. It reminded me of Jenni's lips forming words beyond the soundproof glass in our office.

"You called me," responded the voice I hadn't heard in years outside of old videos I watched sometimes when I felt particularly pitiful.

"Are you Olivia?" I asked, secretly hoping some mystical universe ether could conjure her back in this liminal space.

"Do you want me to be?"

Yes, I wanted to scream, but that felt like losing, so I kept walking. "I like being alone."

There was a long silence before Olivia's voice said, "Then why did you call me?" in a tone I really missed. Her no-bullshit tone for when I was talking out of my ass or being passive-aggressive.

"I didn't," I replied. "Go away."

I climbed faster, wanting whatever this was to be over. We reached the lookout that Olivia and I had hiked toward that day in Colorado. It had ended in an outcropping with what should have been a beautiful view of that portion of the Rockies in all their gold-ridged, autumnal glory. What we hadn't known during the hike was that some clouds had rolled in while we were in the trees, and our destination emerged as a disappointing smudge. There it was again in the anomaly—that foggy, puke-colored impression of the mountains. The path continued out into what looked like empty air. I paused even though I knew it must be safe to walk onward. None of this was real to begin with. We were in some pin tuck of the universe between two fields in Illinois. Still, I couldn't take the next step. I started to turn around, but Olivia's voice said, "You don't want to do that."

"Why? Will you disappear?"

"No."

A breeze rippled through the mountains, and I felt it under my skin, through my marrow. "Why are we here?" It would have been simpler if I could say this was the happiest I had been or the most in love. That day Olivia and I reached this lookout, took cheeky selfies in front of the anticlimactic vistas, sat swigging our water bottles for a little while before hiking back down. I couldn't remember what I felt then, if anything. There were moments that seemed more significant—when Olivia and I first had sex on a rainy day and then held each other in serene silence for an hour afterward; when she told me her diagnosis on an autumn morning so bright I thought I was dreaming. But this moment had been nothing, achingly banal, and that realization was enough to make me want to cry anyway.

"Go on," Olivia's voice urged. "It'll be okay."

"Come with me." My own voice came out humiliatingly thin and broken. "Olivia?"

No answer.

"Please. I'm sorry, I lied. I don't want to go alone."

But Olivia or the entity, or whatever it was, didn't respond again. I asked again, waited again before finally accepting that I came alone and would have to continue on alone, however long it took. I collected myself and took a running start. I intended to jump straight into the mist, but at the very last moment, on the edge that wasn't an edge, I thought of Olivia's twilit-blue face emerging from the dark doorway in the moment she chose, not me. I couldn't let her end it like that once more. My body stumbled on as I twisted back for a glimpse, but I saw it, all of it, just for a moment, that terrifying face with no body and no end, writhing with everything I'd ever feared while lying awake in the dark. I felt a strangling, suffocating horror in its existence that seized up my whole body so completely, I thought my blood would stop running even as I came tumbling onto a field in Illinois at sunset. My skin the same honey hue but different.

Lemon Boy

Angela's mother died one spring when we were in our early twenties, back when Angela was dating Ollie and the three of us lived in that decrepit place in Somerville. Angela inherited her mother's house in Cambridge and had to spend the summer emptying the place before she sold it to overseas developers. I didn't know Angela all that well even though we had lived together for several years, but I remember that cavernous house. Before I saw it, I had no idea her family was wealthy or that her father wasn't in the picture. Ollie met her on Tinder right after college, while he and I were roommates. I saw them at breakfast a few mornings, and something clicked, I guess, because he started bringing her around to parties and bars as his girlfriend. A few months later, Ollie asked if she could move in, and I was happy to pay a little less in rent.

There was nothing offensive about Angela. She was easygoing but obtuse, a good drinker and a good listener. I couldn't bring myself to resent her even after I saw the beautiful place she grew up in, learned that her financial complaints and thrifted clothes were just for show. Her life was extravagant but tragic. I had a whole family to disappoint with my lack of income and ambition, but Angela had only this house, sold to be stripped and subdivided into yet another overstuffed Camberville multiunit.

After setting a closing date, Angela said farewell to her childhood home with a bang in a series of elaborate parties. The first few I missed because I often worked the closing shift at Starbucks and frequently fell asleep in all my work clothes when I got home. I hated myself most for missing the Halloween party—a professionally organized haunted house that our friends would talk about for years after. I had a costume planned and everything but passed out on the couch while waiting for my leftover burrito to microwave. I woke up at eight A.M. the next day to a kitchen that smelled like refried beans for days.

I hated myself a lot in those years. I had a job that humiliated me in small ways every day and a family that found me difficult, if not impossible, to be around. No friends who knew my real thoughts. I performed a facsimile of living for some time before I could figure out how to do it for real again.

With multiple alarms and many ounces of cold brew, I left work determined to attend Angela's pre-Thanksgiving party. The Halloween party had been a bitch to set up and clean up, so for the next one, Angela worked with a group that planned underground parties throughout the city. To this day, I have no idea how she knew of them. I didn't even know there was an underground party scene in

Boston, a sleep-early city built to make partying difficult. I knew I couldn't miss this one. Its theme was *Eyes Wide Shut*—suits and slinky dresses, shiny masks over red lips, satin capes. I heard a rumor that there was some kind of sex room too, but I didn't see it myself, because that night I met Lemon Boy.

Ollie and Angela spent all day at the house setting up, so I planned to meet them there after I finished my shift at eleven. I had invited this guy from work, Liam, because we closed together a lot and he went out of his way to tease me for every little thing—how I held the mop, my elbows when I steamed milk, the way I struggled to pour silver sacks of coffee beans into plastic bins. This meanness passed for flirtation, and I had a feeling he would sleep with me if we were drunk enough. Liam was hot in that sleeve-tattoo-American-Spirits way—attractive but too boring to incite any real feelings, which felt safe. I was too tired and broke to fall in love, but horny despite it all.

At midnight I picked the lint off a Forever 21 bodycon I'd had since high school and threw a lace-and-ribbon mask over my eyes. Sexy but not trying too hard, because I would have rather died than be caught trying too hard for Liam. I took an Adderall and waxed and plucked the loose threads from my best lingerie. Liam told me he'd stop at home to change and then meet me at the party, so I arrived alone.

The house was a magnificent Victorian tucked into a residential street off Mass Ave. I couldn't even imagine how much it must have been worth—I never asked, of course, but I know now it put Angela through grad school at the very least. This was the first night I saw the house in person. I wasn't sure what color it was in daylight, but in the dark it had different shades of gray for siding and trim, a few wobbly stained glass windows. The party was at its height, shadowed heads filling up windows beaming colored lights. A low thrum of bass emerged anytime the front door opened and shut.

As I waited for Liam, I lingered on the wide front porch, where a crowd lounged on mismatched patio furniture with cigarettes and joints. Already people had unbuttoned their stuffy clothes, pushed the masks from their sweaty faces. I leaned on the rail and tried to light up, but the safety was still on my Mini BIC, and the pregame whiskey made my thumb wobble on the button. I dropped the lighter and swore.

"Here." A boy with lemon yellow hair held up his lighter. He stood wedged into the corner of the porch, wearing a white T-shirt and black surgical mask pulled down to his chin so he could smoke. It so missed the mark on the dress code that I had to assume it was intentional. He had a smooth face that looked waxy in the porch light, making it hard to tell his age. I leaned in close to his long fingers, and when I looked up, he was staring right at me with black eyes, the lighter's flame bobbing in each of them.

"How's your night?" I asked after I had a good light going.

"Kind of weird," he said.

"Well . . ." I glanced over my shoulder. "It's a weird party."

"It's not that."

I could tell he wanted to talk, but I didn't mind. Smoking outside a party was like being in a separate miniparty—a little taste of what's inside. And this man stood out so distinctly from the people around him that I wanted to know what could possibly be stranger than him. "What's weird, then?" I asked.

"My ex is here."

I laughed. It was more trivial than I expected. "There are two types of people." I raised two fingers. "Crushes." I put one down. "And Exes." I closed my hand into a fist. "Everyone here is one of them." This is a bit of nonsense I heard from another friend of mine, and I often parroted it with conviction because I liked the violence of words like *crush* and *ex*.

"She's different, though. This ex. It was messy how we left things."

"So she's both a crush *and* an ex?"

"No, she's dead."

I paused. This was a bit heavy. I thought about this girl I went to high school with, who I knew from class and saw at parties because she was friends with some of my friends even though she and I were never close. She died of an overdose while we were in college. I didn't know her enough to go to the funeral or anything, but when I saw the memorial posts piling up on Facebook, I remembered the last time I saw her. It was the summer between freshman and sophomore year of college, and I was leaving a party in the early morning to get McDonald's breakfast with some friends. When I opened the door, she was sitting on the steps outside the back porch, clutching a Marlboro Light and crying. I stepped around her like she wasn't there, and I still think about how we left her like that because we didn't want an awkward conversation to get between us and our

McGriddles. All this is to say that years later, not long before I went to Angela's party, I thought I saw that girl on the train: dyed red hair, thick eyeliner, striped shirt over faded jeans, Hot Topic bracelets on her pale wrists. She hadn't looked like that since she was fourteen, but even then, I was so sure it was her, I almost reached across the crowd to say hello. But then I remembered that it couldn't be her—that I could never run into her on the train because she was dead. The doors opened, and she disappeared into the rush hour crowd like she was never there. I thought maybe this boy saw his ex at this party in the same way. Her, but not her.

"Oh. I'm sorry." I took a drag because I didn't know what else to say.

He shook his head. "No. You don't understand. She's really here. Like, it's actually her. I just don't know how."

I shrugged. "Are you sure she died? Like, maybe it was a rumor or something, and she's actually fine." This was bullshit, of course, because who makes up a rumor about someone dying?

"I was there, though." He flicked his cigarette butt and looked at me. "I watched her die." For a moment, I thought I saw the flame in his eyes again, even though his lighter was safely pocketed and mine was still on the ground. I had this churning feeling like my blood suddenly ran faster through my veins. Lemon Boy pulled up his face mask so only his eyes burned out from beneath his saccharine hair, as if this would keep at bay the shift that had already occurred in my thoughts of him—from wondering *who* he was to *what* he was.

"What do you mean?" I leaned in, alert to the fact that I was about to hear something wild that I could tell Ollie and Angela later.

"I was about to text you!" This was Liam walking up the porch steps with supremely bad timing. "Have you been inside yet?"

"I, uh . . ." I looked back to Lemon Boy, but he was already turning away from me, palm holding open the front door.

"I'm sure I'll see you in there," he said and disappeared into the party within.

The house was beautiful inside too. The staircase by the door was trimmed with intricate carved mahogany judiciously maintained by Angela's mother to look waxed and shiny even months after her death. The living room opened into a dining room empty of furniture and full of bodies. *Stranger Things* was big that year, so the dance floor was dressed like the Upside Down, all black light and painted paper lining the walls, crumpled and twisted streamer fronds dripping from the ceiling. I pulled Liam into the crowd and did some awkward, jokey dance moves to feel out the mood. He laughed and played along, but even as I snapped and tapped in this absurd flirtation, my gaze latched onto every snatch of yellow I caught over his shoulder. I spotted Lemon Boy at last, slipping through the swinging kitchen door. I leaned forward and said into Liam's ear over the music, "I need a drink."

I left him with some chatty people by the fridge and lingered at the kitchen island, scanning the room. On the counter, rows of aluminum trays held egg rolls, crab rangoons, and steamed dumplings.

I put a rangoon in my mouth and regretted it immediately. It was cold and chewy. A girl stood squinting through her mask at a tray of dumplings, slicing each of them open with her acrylic nails and sniffing the exposed lump. Lemon Boy was by the stove, next to a tray of chocolate chip cookies. He pulled down his mask to bite one and then smiled at me. I pushed through the packed kitchen toward him. By the time I reached him, his mask was up again, rippling in the low light as he chewed.

"Any good?" I asked, trying to act casual.

"Stale," he replied. "And dry."

I nodded. "The rangoons are no better."

When he pulled down his mask to put more cookie in his mouth, I got a closer look at his face. It was hard to say if he was attractive. He had an unusually long and sharp face, kind of vampiric, like he might have been typecast as a villain. His nose was so straight it looked unnatural. He seemed like a person I'd be really into if I were drunker but then might deeply regret the next morning. I had to admit there was something alluring about how he held himself with a bit of a slant, though, a kind of feminine posture that curved his lines into something I'd want to touch.

As if hearing my thoughts, he grabbed my arm unexpectedly tight, eyes wide over his mask. He pulled me close. "Stay here for a sec."

"Why?"

"My ex is here."

"Yeah, you told me that before."

"No, she's like *here* here. In this room."

I tried to look over my shoulder, but he tugged me closer to him, pressing my cheek to his neck in a tight, one-armed hug. "No. Don't look at her."

I laughed. "Like, what, I'll turn to stone?" But when I looked at him, the seriousness in his face gave me a chill. He had such dark eyes, I couldn't tell the state of his pupils, whether he was on anything or not. He barely had eyelashes, and this made his look even deeper, an uninterrupted black that was strange under his candy-colored hair.

The music blared then—someone holding the swinging door open. Laughter erupted by the fridge. Someone dropped a beer can, and it rolled noisily over the kitchen tiles. It felt like all the sounds of the party became amplified for a moment, like the swell of strings in a horror film. Instinctively, I grasped the soft fabric of Lemon Boy's T-shirt.

The moment passed as quickly as it had come on. The party fell to an ambient hum, and Lemon Boy loosened his grip on me. "You wouldn't be laughing if you knew," he said at last, looking at me.

I licked the rangoon crumbs off my lips. "Knew what?"

"I don't know if I should tell you."

I touched his waist. The conversation felt intimate, despite my cream-cheese breath. "Tell me."

Lemon Boy moved his hand down my back. He pulled me close again, pushing my face up like he was about to kiss me. Instead he slid his cheekbone against my temple and spoke into my ear in that low secret-voice you use at a party to talk shit about someone who's not far away. "The girl, this girl. I should have never gotten involved with her.

I met her at a concert, just a small, local thing. I went because my friend was in one of the opening acts, and she was in the second opener. She had pink hair then.

Every time I saw her, she had different colored hair.

That night it was pink.

I met her outside while we were all smoking between sets. We were talking in a group together until she turned to me and said, 'There are going to be so many holes in there tonight. Did you know there are holes opening up all around us all the time?'

And I thought, *What the fuck*, you know? But I kept talking to her because she was beautiful in this weird way that I was really into. Sharp little face, big dark eyes, and skin like you've never seen— so silky. And everything about her body looked like it was made of math. Perfect angles, exact proportions.

Sorry, maybe that was strange to say.

Not that I'm objectifying her.

I'm just saying she was beautiful.

Anyway, she smoked her cigarette to the filter and told me that she saw holes everywhere. And had I noticed them too?

Now that she mentioned it, I saw the square openings in the storm drain, the crevices in the pavement, the way people's eyes look around but reflect nothing when they're fucked up and thought, *Sure*. I told her, 'I guess I know what you mean,' because I mean, the night sky. It's just one giant hole, isn't it?

She was so excited when I said that. She grasped both of my hands and said, 'Yes, you get it!' That's when she really started coming on to me, I'm pretty sure, getting touchy and all that. She said, 'Here's a secret. When you're onstage looking down at a crowd, if they're really into the music, the holes start opening up everywhere. Most people are too wrapped up in the music to see it. Some people fall in, but nobody notices. From the stage, though, you can see it all if you look hard. It's the most terrifying thing I've ever seen.'

During the concert, at the height of the best song by the headlining band, when everyone was screaming along, I looked around, just like she asked. But there were so many people. If there was a hole, I couldn't see it from my angle. Some heads dipped below others and seemed to disappear, but that could have been the trick of the crowd.

After the concert, I lingered to smoke, and she came right up to me and asked, 'Did you see them? There were a lot tonight.'

I told her about the disappearing heads because I saw a chance to impress her, and it worked; she was so pumped. She kissed me right there, saying, 'Thank you, thank you. There's nothing worse than being scared alone. I feel like I've been waiting for you all this time so I can be scared with you.'

So of course I brought her home. How could I not? We went out a lot after that. Went to concerts to look for holes. It was a weird little hang-up of hers, but that was the only thing. I thought, *I can live with this.* She was so cute and fun otherwise. But the last concert we went to . . ."

Lemon Boy inhaled sharply then, and the sound sent a shock to my groin. I realized his knee had slid between my legs, and our stomachs were pressed together, me gripping his T-shirt with both hands at his waist like I was ready to yank it off.

I pulled back quickly. "The stove," I said. "I think you hit one of the dials."

This broke the trance, and he was once again a boy with yellow hair, quickly turning around to check each of the knobs along the large stainless-steel stove. I leaned against the island and tugged down my dress. I wasn't sure when we had gotten that close, if he was flirting with me or if this was some weird post-breakup thing he was going through. But I liked the way he touched me as though he'd already seen me naked.

"You should go back to your friend." Lemon Boy nodded at Liam, who was holding two beers and finishing a conversation with some other tattooed brunette. "You seem nice. If I tell you more, you might start seeing holes too. I shouldn't do that to you."

Liam caught sight of me then, and the way he smiled and raised a PBR in my direction felt so achingly normal, I didn't want to rejoin him. When I turned around to find Lemon Boy, he was already gone, absorbed by the slippery atmosphere of the party as if we hadn't just been skin to skin. I wanted to leave Liam behind and follow Lemon Boy. In those days, I longed for nothing more than a party I could sink deep into between work shifts. I really wanted to know what happened to that girl who saw holes, where she sank, and how she resurfaced again at this party, skipping all the in-between things that felt somehow less real.

"Let's go upstairs already," Liam said, coming up to me and pressing the cold can into my hand. I accepted it and looked around, reorienting myself. The girl with the acrylic nails was gone, but every dumpling in the tray had a thin laceration.

"Upstairs?"

"Those guys were just telling me all the rooms are themed, and there's some art piece." Liam sounded excited.

"Oh, cool." My own voice sounded distant. I opened the beer with my fingernail and the hiss of it brought me back to myself, a skin that felt less mine than Lemon Boy's had against the bone and cartilage on my face.

Each of the rooms upstairs was themed around a color. The whole production was impressive. The Gold Room was well lit and full of conversation. It had gold foil pressed to the walls, glittery throws, and gold-rimmed plastic cups stacked around mostly depleted cock-tail pitchers. Empty cups were everywhere, and I was tempted to stick my finger in each to see if my nail would clack against their plastic bottoms or keep going on and on. The Red Room was papered red with scarves over all the lights and had cushions around low tables, where groups of masked people clustered conspiratorially. They fell silent and turned to stare as we took a surveying turn of the room. The Blue Room had an aquarium against one wall and tall, cool-colored lava lamps. I stood watching the lamps for a bit, the bubbles congealing and pulling away, hoping they would eventually form a perfect loop, opening the liquid into something else. They never did. Frustrated, I let Liam pull me on to the next room. The White Room was the largest, with silver trays cluttered with candy dishes. In the corner there was a tall wardrobe full of bottles and a bartender standing at a table against it, making drinks for passersby. I stopped to pee in the attached bathroom and found the counters lined with small makeup mirrors, tilted to face the ceiling. I cupped a round mirror in both my hands and wondered if this too could be a hole. I leaned in until my face slid into frame, but all I saw were my lace-trimmed eyes with a faint white dusting over them. I traced my finger over the glass and gummed whatever residue was left.

I found Liam outside and asked him if he thought we could find molly somewhere even though it would ruin me for my shift the next day. It still felt like there was something between me and the party. I needed to pull away the gauze, and I thought another upper might do the trick.

"I don't know," Liam said, sipping his beer and looking around. "It's pretty late. Is that a good idea?"

What a drag. As boring as the Americana florals and wildcats on his sleeve piece. I must have pouted or done something to show that thought on my face because he shrugged. "Well, I guess why not." Maybe he wanted to impress me, I don't know. We didn't know each other outside the counter, and I was still figuring out how or if we could have fun together.

Is this fun? I wondered as Liam left me to find this guy he knew from school who could help us out. It was supposed to be. I wanted it to be. I told him I would wait in the White Room, but I hit the end of my beer and felt restless again to find Lemon Boy and his ex. I cataloged all the girls with colored hair—one with an orange buzz cut, one with a teal bob—ready to interrogate Lemon Boy as soon as I could find him. I stole away to the Gold Room, but he wasn't there, so I tried to salvage some cocktail. The buzz settled nicely between my nose and scalp, and each time I saw a girl with colored hair, I thought of Lemon Boy's ex. I tried not to make eye contact with those girls. I wasn't superstitious, but it had been a little chilling how Lemon Boy's gaze dragged into darkness when he looked over my shoulder at her. At the same time, I envied her. Maybe those holes she saw weren't something to fear but were a kind of liberation. I imagined one opening in the little round mouth of a gallon jug of milk, the drain in the back sink, under the flip top of the giant garbage bins I had to roll out to the dumpster each evening. Those places that diminished me could become openings for me to fully disappear. I wanted to be able to slip in freely and only emerge at a party with a fridge full of cold beer and a boy who can't take his eyes off me.

I returned to the White Room and sat on a couch covered in what felt like satiny white tablecloth. The teal and orange girls were gone, but now there was a petite girl with purple space buns drinking something out of a Solo cup in one corner. Everyone around me had straight, bright teeth. It started to scare me how everyone was smiling, how those smiles reflected the room and the room reflected the smiles. The bartender had a splotchy red face and seemed to know everyone who walked up even though he looked older than anyone there. After a while I couldn't tell if he was hired to bartend or if he was just a man who wanted to make everyone drinks.

I realized this was the master bedroom the second time I went to pee. Angela's mother had died in this bedroom. I knew it happened at home, in her own bed, in her sleep. I always wondered how Angela handled all these people snorting whatever in the bathroom where her mother had brushed her teeth for the last time, but of course we never talked about it. We would lose touch after she and Ollie break up. In a year, I would meet my boyfriend and get a job at a start-up where I would see the same hundred people at work each day. These were small changes, but they helped. Working at a counter, I was numb to human interaction. I saw stranger after stranger without cataloging a single feature. In some ways, the world was bigger, more terrifying.

I washed my hands and checked my lipstick in the mirror. With lace mask and bright mouth, I looked completely vacant, like a mannequin. At night I could be undressed and discarded, utterly dispensable. I thought about the holes, how maybe Angela had arranged this party to be just that—a thing that swallowed her mother's fingerprints before the developers could touch them, a place where her childhood could safely disappear. I traced my hand on the marble sink and wondered if anyone would notice if I went with it.

Lemon Boy was not in the Blue Room nor the Red. Lastly, I tried the one door I hadn't yet crossed. Beyond was a tiny room that might have been an office or a nursery once. Projectors cast colored patterns across each wall. Next to the door hung a framed plaque with background about the artist and the installation, but I don't remember what it said. The room was empty except for Lemon Boy sitting in the corner, head against the wall and knees up.

"I found you," I said, surprised at my own relief.

"Why did you come looking for me?"

"I have to know." I stood between him and the images dancing across the opposite wall. "What color is your ex's hair tonight?" As if that would answer everything.

"I don't want to tell you," he replied.

"What if I want to see the holes?" I knelt in front of him. "I'm not afraid," I said, putting my hands on his knees and gulping his bottomless gaze with mine. "Where did she go? Why did she come back here now?" This was no longer a curiosity or something I could retell. The story yawned open before me, itself a kind of hole I wanted to fall into. I wanted all of this to be about me somehow. For Lemon Boy to tell me that his ex was here for me alone, to take me away. I cupped his cheeks the same way I had held the little mirror in the bathroom, asking it to show me something unexpected. "Tell me the rest."

His knees fell apart, his feet sliding down on either side of me. He grasped my hips, thumbs against pelvis, and pulled me closer.

He spoke again in that low voice even though we were alone. "Okay. This is where it gets weird.

Right before the last concert, she looked strange. I couldn't tell if she had worn too much eyeliner or if she had been losing sleep, but her eyes looked different. Her hair a dark red color you don't want to see on anyone's head. When I asked her what was wrong, she said, 'They're getting bigger.' I asked if she wanted to go home, but she shook her head and told me, 'It's worse there.'

We went to the concert even though I wasn't really feeling good about it. It was a DJ set type of show, music made with samples. The artist was covered in neon-and-pastel shapes from a projector, kind of like this room. Sometimes the screen behind him played little clips of cartoons, skinny girls with bright colored hair. My ex's mood contradicted the upbeat, funky music. Everyone around us was dancing. She drank a few expensive drinks and sort of swayed but hardly smiled. Halfway through the show, she started to cry.

I wanted to take her outside for a smoke, anything to get her out, but there was no reentry, and she didn't want to leave. There was something about that night that frightened her, I think. It wasn't hot or cold; there was a dark moon, no stars. The kind of night you can't feel on your skin.

In the bathroom, I pulled her into the big stall and asked what had changed. She told me that nothing had, and that was the problem. The holes had been growing for a while, but she hadn't said anything, hoping that it was a temporary thing. I think she used the word 'fluctuate.' But that morning she realized clearly that it would always be the same, the holes growing, nobody seeing them except me.

'I thought we were going to be scared together,' I told her, and asked the question that had been weighing on me all night: 'Am I not enough?'

She got angry then, saying, 'When is a single person enough for anything?'

I was pretty hurt by that, so I said something I maybe shouldn't have, something like, 'This concert seems to be reaching that point, the one that opens up the dance floor.' I was bullying her, but I couldn't help it. It felt like she was breaking up with me.

And she screamed then, she screamed, 'I know!' and I had to shush her because I didn't want to get kicked out. In hindsight, maybe it would be better if we had, but at the moment my instinct was to go, 'Shhhh' loudly over her words. I asked her, 'Why are you doing this?' and she said, 'The problem is, I'm not afraid anymore—and ever since they started growing and growing. And I realized it's not the same for you, is it? You said you see them, but you don't, not really.'

She left the bathroom, but I lingered in the stall and took a quick piss before following her back out. Usually I could find her in a moment by her hair color, so distinct from all the black, brown, and gold, but the lights were flashing all kinds of colors, so it was hard to tell.

The music reached a fever pitch. The DJ started one of his hits, and everyone sang along to the sample that said, 'I wanna be with you.'

I finally found her head between the gaps in people's arms. She no longer looked desperate but completely blank. The crowd swayed her side to side, and she sank with each motion. All of a sudden I could see the holes for real, just like she always said. Holes and holes and holes, puckering. I reached for her between the limbs, caught her under the arms. It was sucking her in, but I couldn't tell where because her hips were caught between two people, and the lower half of her body disappeared behind them. I asked her to help, but she stayed limp. Finally, I really put my legs into it and yanked with my waist, twisting and wrenching, and that's when her torso ripped clean off her bottom half, which quickly disappeared into the crowd. I screamed, but it was drowned out by a chorus of 'YOU.' I was sure then that she was dead. Her eyes were open, her mouth was open, but she was just a body riddled with useless, empty openings. I was sweating a lot, and the next time someone jostled me, I lost grip of her. She got sucked in between people's shins and disappeared. I waited all night for the venue to empty, but I never found her or any trace of blood on the floorboards.

I thought I wanted to forget about her, but I keep showing up to these places—the kind that might be full of holes. And of course she always shows up like this."

Lemon Boy had his cheek on my neck, his lips moving against the curve of my shoulder. I still don't understand why this story brought our bodies closer, his thighs clenched around my hips. I felt an ache between my legs and arched my back just a little as he moved his hands, damp and warm, around my rib cage with spread fingers. I loved the way his bones mirrored mine in that moment. I could wait until the morning to hate myself for this. I slid my hand between my shoulder and his cheek and raised his head. I wanted to lean down and kiss him, but when he looked up at me, his unnatural yellow hair pressed to his forehead where it had just been stuck to my neck, I couldn't stop thinking about his ex. Did he dye his hair after she was gone or while he was with her? In this room full of undulating patterns, his half-open mouth looked both empty and writhing. Neither of us closed the distance between our lips until finally, I said, "I need a cigarette."

"Let's go downstairs, then. To the basement. There's something I want to show you."

The basement was unfinished and felt most like a party I'd been to before. Creaky wooden stairs led to dark cement that was full of boxes and odds and ends, a crowd blooming under the single row of fluorescent lights. People sat on whatever was around; there was a group of girls on the laundry machines. I didn't know if it was officially designated or unofficially occupied, but this was the smoking room for those who didn't want to brave the November cold. In a year or so, vapes would become more popular, but at the time having one was still a little silly, something for teenagers or a particular type of asshole, so we all stewed there in a mist of tobacco and weed. Someone had a speaker set up in the corner, playing a hip-hop track that ran discordant to whatever beat pulsed down from upstairs. I stood awkwardly with a cigarette between my lips, waiting for

Lemon Boy to light it, but he wandered away into a darker part of the basement without offering. I knew he wanted me to follow him, but I wasn't ready yet, so I leaned against the side of the washing machine and asked one of the girls for a light.

She flicked open a Zippo and said, "Better than asking one of the guys, right?"

I leaned in and nodded. "Always an invitation."

When she turned back to her friend, I hovered for a bit, puffing and wondering whether I should have sought out an invitation after all. I was never good at starting conversation. I once worked for a catering company for a single night and had to quit the next day. Walking up to crowds with trays of food was so stressful, I cried for an hour after my shift was over. That's why I had worked at Starbucks for so long instead of opting for something with better tips—the counter provided a degree of security, a certainty in what words could pass over it. It's why I brought Liam to the party and clung to Lemon Boy once I found him. There was something horrific about facing a party alone. It made you both invisible and vulnerable at once.

The basement people were beginning to look inhuman in the weird fluorescent half-light. When they laughed, their teeth gleamed, and their tongues looked raw and bloodied. All unfinished New England basements have this in-between quality, gray and damp and spidery, but this one felt particularly so with the party thumping above and a deep silence seeping up from the ground below. I couldn't be sure if these creatures were partygoers turned monstrous in the liminal atmosphere, or things that had always been here, just below Angela's little-girl feet. They didn't see me; I didn't want to see them. This is why I finally walked into the shadows after Lemon Boy. I caught a glimpse of his yellow hair farther into the dark and followed it. I took his hand when I got close enough and asked, "What did you want to show me?"

"You don't see it?"

I waited a little while, taking drags until my eyes adjusted. The back wall was broken into and dug out like an animal had burrowed there. The concrete walls crumbled into dark earth. There seemed to be nothing on the other side, the blackness stretching out like Lemon Boy's eyes.

"Is this one of your ex's holes?" I whispered, my voice shrinking before this tunnel.

"I don't know," he whispered back. "But for some reason, it doesn't scare me."

"What do you think is inside?"

"Honestly," he said, "nothing."

We stood facing it for a few more seconds before he let go of my hand. I grabbed for the hem of his shirt and said, "Don't."

"I have to. This is where she wanted me to end up, I think." He turned to me, but I couldn't really see his face, just rinds of his yellow hair catching what little light they could. "She's waiting for me."

I could have asked him to take me with him. I'm certain he wanted me to. He would have taken my hand and pulled me straight into the thick of it. I was struck then by the enormity of this discovery. I had pushed back a veil between my world and the infi-nite, dreadful things that were not supposed to be possible. To keep going would be to rip the veil down entirely, be vulnerable forever. "I'll wait for you," I said instead, releasing his shirt reluctantly.

"Sure." He nodded. "I'll be right back."

Lemon Boy crawled in, taking a few paces on his knees before the ground leveled and he was able to stand upright. He walked deeper into the tunnel and soon disappeared. I stood on the precipice of this small abyss and saw clearly all the openings in the world, the flimsy places that people could fall into and never really return. Be here but not here. I had toed this line many times but never had it in me to step in. I was scared then, and I'm scared still of that dark place I saw again and again in those years. The memory sits like a cool stone in my mind at all times—black, smooth, and terribly beautiful. Maybe that fear is what keeps us tethered until the world finally closes around us in the fresh drip of dawn.

I stomped out my cigarette without waiting to see what, if any-thing, came out of that hole. I left the party through the bulkhead doors and walked home alone.

After that night I couldn't find anyone who knew Lemon Boy or had even seen him. Angela and Ollie both said I didn't make it to the party at all since I was already asleep when Ollie returned the next morning without running into me at Angela's house once. I could have described all the details of the night to make them believe me—the colored rooms, the Upside-Down dance floor, all things I heard other people talk about when they told their own stories from that party—but I wasn't sure I wanted to find out if that hole in the basement was really there or not. Liam didn't mention the party when I saw him at work the next day, and he gave me the cold shoulder from then on because I ditched him, I think. He probably paid good money for some molly we never got to do. Shortly after, he moved cities without answering my goodbye text. When I got a new phone and lost our text history, it was almost a relief because I could really believe I had never been at that party.

For a while I felt like Lemon Boy had left me with some kind of curse, had tied a thread between me and that other place. Every time I saw a girl with colored hair, I got tense and goose bumped. As each day waned, I kept expecting holes to start growing all around me like some kind of invasive flora, but they never did. Finally, I dyed my hair entirely hot pink to shake myself out of it. This worked for the most part, but I never forgot how Lemon Boy sank into that viscous darkness like he belonged there or how close I was to following him. There are still times when I open the door and the day is agape, the night sky a mouth.

Supergiant

I t's the last night of my last tour, and all I want is to tell my makeup
artist I love her. In the venue's cellarage, it's just the two of us. The
roar of the crowd outside is so absolute, it melts into a shimmer of
white noise. Less emerges doll-like from the gaping dark, bright and
unreal like a candy-colored hologram. She is pink today, just like she
was the first day we met. Every show she comes head to toe in one
bright hue—hair, nails, lipstick, clothes—so I can spot her easily
even with my pupils still constricted tight for the stage lights. She
must have done this color on purpose, a sentimental gesture, but I
hate how it feels like she's closing the loop on our time together. All
the tender words I spent days preparing die in my mouth. Instead I
say, "I'm hungry, Less."

"Of course," she says, her look as blank as ever. "You worked hard."

"How was I tonight?" I ask as she hands me a towel for my
damp neck.

"Radiant." Less says this every time, though I'm not sure she's ever seen me perform.

I wanted this night to be different. My fans don't know it was my last performance, and I wasn't allowed to give them any clues. I made only one deviation in my set—a final act of rebellion—when I broke the encore choreography. Instead of running back and forth with one arm raised and waving during the chorus, I went to the very edge of the stage and reached out as far as I could. Even with the six feet of aisle, a metal barricade, and black-clad security between me and the audience, the crowd came to an unprecedented frenzy. This was as close as I'd ever been to them. I shivered with the thrill of it, a flinch I hoped wouldn't show on the forty-foot screens projecting my glowing face. All those faraway eyes just beyond reach, the sweaty palms and wrists covered in multicolor bracelets spelling my name, polished nails holding neon painted posters professing their love. I imagined flinging myself into their arms. I wanted them to scream inside me, claw my guts the way they clawed the air between us. Fill me up the way birds and insects fill an airless summer night. But of course the show ended like any other. The last thing I said onstage was *I can't wait to see you all again.*

Less and I walk through the web of painted black poles and wires below the stage. This underbelly is our private domain. We weave expertly through the dark, knowing just when to drift close and when to come apart. Nobody else is allowed to be this close to me. When I signed with the label a decade ago, they explained very clearly what happened next: the procedure would make me so perfect I'd be untouchable. One of those celebrities with flawless skin and bright eyes who were never seen in person. A face so beautiful you could lose your mind.

I agreed because I had no idea what it was like to be dismantled and recomposed. I was eighteen. The seaside town I lived in before had nothing to offer but a placid life that kept some people sane and made others squirm, the waves breaking and breaking like a metronome over our days. Growing up in a place like that keeps you naive for longer. I arrived at the audition after a four-hour bus ride, desperate and pliable. Squirming.

Sometimes I try to imagine the life I might have had in that town, working days at the family restaurant and spending evenings hip to hip with someone at a crowded bar. I would have been loved less but held more. I don't know if I'm happier with how things turned out or if happiness really matters. I chose to live craving, aching for another person's touch, waking up cold in different beds every day. But in any life, I would have ached for something. Each time I step in front of a crowd, feel the air hum with their cries, I know, I know I'd do it all again.

Less is the exception. She's the only breathing thing I've touched since then, and I know her body like my own. Even in the dark I could draw her outline from the way the air changes as she takes each step. I reach for her hand now, and she curls her fingers around mine one by one in that strange way that reminds me she's not human. I don't know what she is or why she can come right up to my face even when I'm fresh out of a performance. I've never asked questions because I didn't want to risk changing anything between us.

"What are you in the mood to eat?" Less asks in the dressing room as she unmakes me. I came to love her because of this intimacy, I think: her hands in my mouth, undoing the seams, peeling back the skin around my synthetic bones. She takes away my celebrity skin and presses on something more common, more like the features I was born with, which were so unexceptional, I hardly remember them.

We're in a city I've never seen beyond the stage, the back hallway, my tinted-window van, and the hotel suite. "Something new," I say. "I want tonight to be special."

Less doesn't respond right away. I open my eyes and find her back to me, facing the performer skin draped in its case. I'm pretty sure it's the last time we'll see it. The label told me that if I keep going, the skin will be past its prime. It'll age and wither like any other. They'd rather cut things short now, before I fade and sour. I accept this ending because I know it's better to be remembered at my best. This face was never really mine to begin with. I reach around Less to touch its cheek, my gleaming fingernails next to her rosy ones.

"Does it make you feel anything?" Less asks me.

"Not really. It's hollow."

Less has never asked me anything like this before. She's always cool, efficient. Cheerful in a subdued way that calms me. Our ending hits me the way endings only do at the threshold, when you're nose to nose with it. Less closes the lid and latches the case. If she feels anything, she doesn't want to show me. I don't know if she feels anything ever. She turns to me with a serene smile. "Okay. Let's do something special."

The view from my suite is the best in the city. The skyline is cradled and secret in heavy clouds, the honeycomb of lit windows leaving an afterglow in the overcast haze. Neon signs in a pictographic language I can't read flicker all around. From my bed, I watch the "live" video I recorded from this hotel room years ago. My stage face smiles while I wear a fluffy robe and wave. I interact only with the most generic comments that are sure to pop up every time. Yes, I love you too. This is what I ate. This person designed my costume. Tomorrow, I fly to the next city. My adult life has been a string of prerecorded posts like this, my busy schedule the standing excuse for virtual interviews and declined appearances. At the end I yawn and grin and stretch out my fingers in a wave. *I'm so tired after all the fun we had. I'll see you in the morning,* and then the stream goes dark. Millions of viewers leave a flurry of disappointed comments, plead for me to stay longer, but my life is already over. Tomorrow the reports of my tragic, untimely death will surface, and that will be the end.

The hours after a show are difficult for me. There are no after-parties, no nights out in celebration, no messy tour hookups. Just me and the ceiling above an unfamiliar bed. Emptiness overtakes me as I go through a kind of withdrawal. The world is crisp onstage, every light a sharp thing that almost pricks me. Once it's over, my whole sense of self wobbles. I don't know who I am offstage. This body doesn't feel like it's mine when it's unchoreographed. I can't even describe how jarring it was to wake up one day and move through the world in an entirely different vessel. Sometimes I don't feel human either. It's worse this time because there are no more stages to look forward to—only these murky, interstitial spaces that make me feel sick.

Less has always stayed with me through these moments, waiting for me to settle. On most nights we ordered in, watched TV, and ate until the feeling ebbed away, then said our good nights. Tonight she leads me out to the balcony instead. We wait for the rooms around us to turn yellow, blue, then black as the tour staff sinks into sleep. The air is hot and thick with a coming storm, but that doesn't stop us from quietly putting on our shoes once we're sure nobody will notice us leave.

On our way out, Less puts makeup on my plain face to make it look more distinguished. It's nothing like what I wear onstage—just a touch of foundation, little eyeliner streaks applied in the hallway by the door. Her fingers are gentle. As she applies a dab of colored balm, I want to bite them. Her wide magenta eyes flick around as she works, and I wonder how they look without colored contacts. This must be love, I concluded a few months ago: to want to walk beside someone until I can't walk anymore, to want to know everything about her, to want and want. That's what all the songs I've recorded tell me anyway, the words everyone sings back loudest at my shows.

In the elevator, I reach for Less's hand, and she adjusts her bag to let me take it. She's never once pulled away.

Our hotel is in the busy city center. Even at this hour, cabs and buses roar by, and groups of people laugh and call out to one another in the street. After an initial surge of nerves, I realize nobody's noticed me. We brush through the crowd without really being perceived. This is how it'll be from now on. I don't exist. I can do whatever I want, be a stranger in every room I step into. I don't doubt my family thinks I'm lost or dead by now, given the way I left a note on the kitchen table that said, *Going to see if I can make it out there. I'll be back when I can.* I wasn't of course. Even if I showed up at my own mother's door, she wouldn't recognize me. There's barely anything left of the person who grew in her womb, just a bit of organ tissue, a few nerve endings. I'm so utterly free it's paralyzing.

"Where are we going?" I walk closer to Less.

Less releases my hand and puts her arm around me. She can always sense when I need comfort. "The kind of place I used to go to a lot right before we started working together," she says. "Where I learned to act human." We turn off the main drag into narrower and narrower streets. The groups of people thin to twos and threes, still talking, but in subdued tones without traffic sounds to muffle their conversations. The last street opens into a plaza with a maze of stalls covered in tarp awnings, each with its own digital sign flashing what Less says are menu items, sometimes with discounts. Customers gather on clusters of plastic furniture. The stalls mostly serve food, a few bar counters and shop fronts, one little arcade, buskers peppered here and there. I squeeze Less's arm, smiling wide. I've never felt so part of the world, a place I had lived but not lived in until now. "I knew you'd like it," Less says, squeezing me back.

We settle on a stall with rows of skewered meat and mounds of fluffy, colored rice. We sit elbow to elbow with the people eating around us. "What's better," Less asks once we've passed the initial stage of wordlessly enjoying a long-awaited meal, "a crowd like this that's close enough to feel or the crowds at your shows that are far enough to see in full? I've always wondered what it's like to be onstage."

"You're full of questions tonight," I reply, unsettled. Everything Less knows about me has been volunteered during our late-night meals and car rides and layovers. She's always accepted but never solicited details about my past, my likes and dislikes. Her new curiosity feels like a key change before the last chorus. Our goodbyes already waxing.

She shrugs. "Before, I thought you'd tell me everything eventually."

I feel a little embarrassed by this, like I overshare.

"But now," she continues, "I have to ask just in case."

"There's still time. We have all the time."

Less looks down at her food, and I can't tell if she feels bad or awkward. I don't know what she'll do now that my career is done.

Will they assign her to the next talent, then the next? She's still impossible to read, despite how I've always been unfurled before her like a long and inky scroll.

"Why don't you tell me something about yourself instead," I say, wanting to change the subject.

"There's nothing to tell," she replies. "Or nothing you'd want to know."

"I want to know everything," I say, maybe too quickly.

She gives me a pitying smile. "No, you don't."

I look at our almost-empty plates. I don't like her nonanswers, how even tonight she won't give. Dread descends swiftly, and with it a downpour of rain. The water hits the tarp thunderously, and the voices around us swell in response. The night has amplified, hit a crescendo. Coated in slick reflections, the city is wounded and bleeding. The musty scent of damp grime smothers the market fragrance of sweat and oil and grilled meat.

"The city is washing off its makeup," Less says, gazing at the spattering edges between tarps, dark lines already forming below the cracks.

"What does it look like when it's barefaced?"

"A beast," Less says with no hesitation. "We're all beasts underneath."

"Even you?"

She takes a sip of her tea without answering and stands up. "I'm done. I'm going to return my plate. What about you?"

I nod. My appetite is gone by now. As Less walks away with our trays, a little pink ember in the crowd, the air collapses from my chest. This can't be all there is between us.

I leave our lukewarm tea on the table and walk into the rain.

I'm not sure which way we came, so I duck into the closest alley. I'm soaked through before the market is even out of sight. Water seeps into the cracks of this cheap skin. The label made it for sleeping and sitting inside, not this kind of exposure. The streets are mostly empty now, but I still feel watched. Feline eyes gleam from corners; blurry silhouettes hover in lit windows. A man stands alone under an awning with a bulging jute sack cradled in his arms, following me with his whole head as I pass. I take erratic turns. I think I want to be lost. I've never been lost in my life. In my hometown I knew every road, all named after trees and sea things and men. In the rest of the world I've only known a few rooms.

I turn the corner and see a house with a window cracked open, a teenager with their back to me, running a curler through their hair. I can only see a shoulder and half a face through the mirror. A long time ago that was me—painstakingly separating each strand, twirling and arranging it just so. I was both unremarkable and vain. One time I asked my manager on a call why he chose me for this project. He was quiet for a long time, before saying, *You must know.*

I said, *Tell me anyway.*

He said, *Because you were the least interesting person who auditioned. You had absolutely nothing to give but wanted everything.*

I step into the archway of their house and stand over a glossy, undisturbed puddle pooling in from the street. I crouch down and stare into it under the white light of the nearest streetlamp. The makeup Less painted on so tenderly has been reduced to faint smears on my cheeks. I search and search my reflection for some sense of who I once was. What kind of person has nothing to give? I wonder if I become her again every time I step out of the spotlight. Maybe the pit that opens inside me postperformance isn't emptiness, just my vacuous true self spilling back in.

The corners of my mouth and the little divot where my earlobe meets my jaw are beginning to peel. These cheekbones were made for my performance face, so nothing else stays on for very long. Even if they gave me back my original face, it wouldn't fit. I open my mouth wide, unlock my jaw with a push from the heel of my hand, and swallow my fingers. I fumble behind my teeth for all the fastenings, leaning against the archway as I shove my hands farther. At last they come undone. I leave the empty face on the ground like a warning. The teenager is at the window now. They see me, and their face contorts. I dart away, knowing how I must look: a fleshy body with a skeleton face. A kind of beast. I laugh a little at how comically horrifying I am. I like it.

Around the corner I come face-to-face with two young girls. One screams and grabs for her friend. I slip quickly into an alley. They have a quick exchange in a language I don't understand, one girl frightened while the other one sounds surprised. A long pause. A calmer exchange, then nervous giggles.

The girls walk by, and I press close to the shadows until their split-splat steps melt completely into rain sounds. I laugh again. I run through the paths, following them uphill, away from the main road. I jump out at passersby and disappear again just when they've seen me. I stand in front of windows until I startle someone. I relish the way everyone's faces come open in new, frantic expressions. This could be my next life. I imagine living off scraps in the alleys until I merge with them, becoming something mythic. Is there a difference between fear and worship? Either way they'll lie in bed thinking of me. Even when a new celebrity plasters the billboards with their glossy face, I'll linger here at night. Each time a person walks more quickly between two streetlights, I'll be born again. Between my wet footfalls, I hear my manager's voice again, the dark way he said *everything*.

I don't know how long I've been walking when, without warning, everything goes black: a power outage. For a moment I panic. The alleys are narrow, and the houses take menacing shapes in the unfettered night. The city falls quiet as if saying, *Enough. It's over.* The rain fills the absence of mechanical sound. I stumble onward as flickering candle flames drift in the windows around me like little ghosts. I emerge in an empty square with one lonely fountain. At its center, a sculpture of sharp-toothed animals spits water into a rippling bowl. Less sits on the rim, her eyes gleaming like a predator's in the dark. I'm so relieved to see her, the pink dawn at the end of a long dream.

"How did you find me?" I ask.

"Of course you'd walk right into the heart of the city. You always want to be at the center of things." She stands on the lip of the fountain. "Come with me."

Less climbs the sculptures, her limbs moving with fluid, insectile finesse. I follow steadily, my body conditioned for hours onstage. We find easy footing on glistening stone snouts, haunches, and curved spines. Polished tigers midroar, howling dogs, a thick ribbon of a dragon, plumed birds with curved beaks and wild eyes. Less comes to rest on the dragon's head and I on a wing.

"Look at that," she says, pointing. A ring of black surrounds us—the darkened district—and beyond it the rest of the city burns bright like a strange shoreline. Look at that. The town I was born in rested on a cove. On clear nights, from the perfect center of the beach, the coast curled in upon you just like this, a bright knife cutting apart the sea. At its very tip, a lighthouse pulsed all night.

"Should we go home now?" I ask.

"You have no home," Less says. "You know that."

"I was born somewhere."

"But you were born again."

When I first came out of the haze of drugs that followed my surgery, I was in a small apartment the label had prepared for me. They had left my new face on so it could settle over the reshaped bones and placed my bed before a fully mirrored wall because they knew. I pressed myself close to the reflection. Fuck, I was so perfect. I stripped naked and examined every corner of my body. I touched myself all night, all over, kissed the cold mirror, and licked my fresh skin. I wasn't born again; something else was born instead.

Less reaches into her bag and takes out the case that keeps my stage face. "Let's do it one last time."

"Isn't it dangerous out here?" I glance around, but the square is an empty racket of raindrops on stone.

"You'll be safe with me." She opens the box. "Come here."

Less puts a hand on my exposed skull and traces the line of my molars to the hinge by my ear. I open my mouth slightly, letting her thumb in to slide against my tongue. With her other hand, she puts four fingers between my incisors and applies pressure until my jaw begins to widen, then unclick. Her hand on my ear moves up to cup the back of my neck, pulling me toward her, tilting my head back. I open my legs and arch my back, and she slides over the smooth stone until there's no space left between us.

"You're full of water," she whispers. "All the way down your throat and in your rib cage."

I nod. I'd felt the rain trickling in and weighing me down.

"You're going to die."

She says this gently, like it would mean something to me, but it doesn't. I'm not sure I was ever alive. The girl who spent afternoons walking along the beach in bare feet is as much a myth as the one who blew kiss after kiss to a screen in an empty hotel room. An untouchable thing that leaves no imprint. When I turned my back on the crowd for the last time and lowered slowly from the stage, all that waited for me below was nothing, and Less. This is the only ending that makes sense.

I grip the case tightly where it's wedged between two stone shoulders, not wanting it to slip away while she works. We're balanced precariously, our bodies locked together at what feels like the tip of everything. Less fastens my face back on with slow care, less clinical than usual. When she's done, she slides her hand half out, and I close my lips around her fingers. As she locks my jaw back into place, I lick each of them. This is as close to sex as I've ever been with anyone but myself, and Less accepts it without complaint or pleasure.

She pauses for a moment, thumb resting on my bottom lip, the pads of her fingers on my nose, cheek. "There you are."

"I love you," I tell her.

"Really?" She laughs. "That's so fucking sad."

"What are you?"

"You still don't know? I'm you with nothing inside."

I always wondered what had happened to my face, my bones, my body. I thought they must've been thrown out, not repurposed into whatever Less is. I take her face in both my hands, run my fingers along her skin the same way she did every time she took me apart and put me back together. It's true she's not beautiful. But she's familiar and soft. Her cheeks are full of flesh that I've always wanted to touch like this. She never gave me a thing, but maybe you don't have to give to be loved. She was there, and that was enough.

"Can you feel anything?" I ask.

"Your hands."

"No. Like, inside." I was always searching for signs.

"Not like you do."

I pull her close and press my face against her neck, her strawlike pink wig. "What will happen to you now?"

"I guess when you die, I will too. That seems right."

I nod and inhale deeply. She smells like lotion and salt. I remember a young girl who emerged from a country bus with sand stuck to her heels. Stood in an audition queue for hours, sweating off her sunscreen, practicing her smile. The way the sun met her face when she walked out, clutching the callback sheet like she was worth something. "Should I be sorry?" I ask her.

"I don't know," Less replies. "Are you?"

Over her shoulder, the hazy city blinks back to life, shrinking the dark ring around us until we emerge spotlit by the lamps around the fountain. I think of my adoring fans raising their lights toward me in the stadium. I'll never know how long they'll mourn me, for how long they'll wake up to my face on their screens and bedroom walls until they move on. But swaying along with my arms, my torso, they brought me to life. We screamed together like one animal, and maybe they'll remember that feeling in their throats.

"How was I?"

Less puts her fingers in my hair and holds tight. "You did well. You were radiant."

"I know." I press closer, as if we could be unraveled and reassembled again if I just hold her tightly enough. "I know, I know."

Nip

Some of me will always be stuck to that hotel room quilt, pinned by those button seals that stitch the corners together. Satin rose mouth. Threadbare fingers. They touch the bare weight of Lucy's thigh as she tries to yank the tucked-in top sheet from between the mattress and frame. Just enough space to get in underneath.

We rent the same room every year, my sometimes-lover and I. There must be residue of me on every wall by now. She, a journalist, knows hotels like her own house. She never books ahead, just drives along roads in our destination until she purses her lips together and taps a clear-coated nail against the wheel, saying, "Mm, yes. That one will do."

This is how we came upon the white vinyl place at the edge of the Cape, the right hook into the Atlantic's chin. You can feel the ocean everywhere; it is so much a part of the air. The curtains are a little yellowed, but we like this, the wall-to-wall carpeting that smells like memories—that's how she describes it. Personally, I don't like to smell. Or hear or see. I don't like being corporeal for very long at all, and she knows this, but once a year I do it for her. I become blood and bone for her as a treat, but I'm not too good at it, which is why I leave trails of me behind everywhere, especially in that bed. She lies between the cheap but at least freshly laundered sheets and waits for me to accumulate beside her. Lips and eyelashes. Follicles and wet openings.

"Hello, stranger," she says.

I smile. If nothing else, I do like to taste, as long as it tastes like her.

She found me in a hotel too. She was twenty-two and had just seen the best concert of her life so far. She had one pressed pill of ecstasy and a lot of vodka, and on that dance floor, she had seen a woman in a cast command hundreds of limbs back and forth like a strobing sea. The city was wide and rapturous outside the hotel room. Her friend had ordered every item on the room-service menu, and they sat on the carpet for a while marveling at the fans of french fries and salad flowers of tomato, lettuce, and fruit, the hazard orange spread of buffalo wings. They touched everything but ate none of it. Once her friend fell asleep, Lucy drew a bath, and I met her gleaming limbs folding into the water. She saw my little bottle and snatched me up and held me to the light and drew in her breath. "I love you," she told me. "I'm in love with you."

All I had known until then was a shelf, a plastic bag, her friend scattering me and other little nips throughout the hotel room as surprises. Lucy's gracefully dilated pupils are the first and last beautiful thing I will ever see.

She graduated college not long after this, and I lived in her purse for years. After being a barista for nine months out of school, she took the tabloid job because it was the only gig she could find with her degree. We got to know each other during those endless stakeouts. I had no senses, but I felt her voice, the way its particular frequency vibrated all through me. She placed me on the dashboard and told me about her life—mother, father, their yellow house that had a yellow lawn no matter how hard her father tried to grow it green.

"My mother told me the grass was just jealous of the house," she said, "and I believed her. I think I still believe her even though it was probably just bad soil. Colors can feel; that's why they make us feel. If I love a color enough, it can love me back." And that's when I realized that I loved her back too.

Lucy was twenty-four when she first tried to pour a little bit of me onto the sheets beside her, and I tried my hardest to become something that could hold her back. I wanted to reciprocate all the times she'd tucked me right between her bra cup and her breast, nestled warm. She was frightened at first. She scrambled off the bed holding the bottle to her chest until I calmly said, "Don't worry. It's just me." As we came pupil to pupil in that low lamplight, she recognized me, saw our nights together pour out in my smile, and smiled back.

Now Lucy is thirty, and we are in love. We walk through the seaside street hand in hand. "We're on island time," she tells me when I ask her what she wants to do. "Let's just walk."

We're not on an island, but I know what she means. It's summer, and Lucy tells me summer smells different from winter—better. I believe her even though it's the only smell I've known. When I open my mouth to the wind, I think I taste joy, but she says it's only spray sunscreen. At a patio table we order a pitcher of beer that pops its way down my throat. I show my pearly teeth. We kiss over fried clams that she eats most of.

I know I'm not the only one. Sometimes Lucy goes into houses or bars or restaurants and leaves me in the car, a dark clatter in her glove compartment. Each year she touches me with nimbler fingers, quicker tongue, a proficiency that only comes with practice, but I don't mind. We're happy. She tells me she saves some secrets for only me, and I believe her, and that is enough.

We save karaoke for last, when we are giddy and fanning ourselves. It's a time of year when sweat clings to the back of Lucy's neck, little peach pearls under the colored lights. I expect them to be cool and gelatin under my fingertips but they're warm, and suddenly it's skin to skin, sticky. She rolls her head along my arm and puts her face against my shoulder. "Do you want to sing something?"

I only know the words to three songs that Lucy plays on repeat when she's driving down a dark road, eyes shiny and fixed: a song by White Lies that she says isn't in the book, some death metal number that I couldn't coax from my throat if I tried, and "Dreams" by The Cranberries. She comes onstage with me and wraps her arm around my waist. We scream into the mic together, all the *la la la ah la*'s, and the bar screams along. We sound awful, but karaoke is when we are most human, our full-throated cries cast into a room full of people who cry back. The thin shirt I borrowed from Lucy is damp, and I realize the whole bar is wet, the ceiling beaded up with condensation, and this feels intimate. She kisses me on the lips as the song's last vocalizations trail off, and everyone cheers. We step offstage, born again.

This is when a man turns toward us at the bar, grins at Lucy, and says, "Hello, stranger."

Lucy's grip on my arm slackens. I see our faces in the mirror behind the bar—we look stricken, slapped. Lucy can't take her eyes off him. We've never met anyone Lucy knows in this little town. It's so far from her nomadic life following celebrities all over the opposite coast, and the often-Airbnb'd apartments we share.

"It's been a while," Lucy says. "This is . . ."

She looks at me; I look at her. We've never given me a name. We always just write *Lucy* on the karaoke sign-up sheet. "Dolores," she says at last.

I don't like that name, but it's too late; it's mine. "Lo," I say, trying to soften the blow of its syllables.

"Is that why you picked that song?" He laughs, and I see his teeth, imperfect, one chipped, and my insides clutch like I'm shriveling. He carries all the signs of a body lived in: bitten nails, hair jutting here and there because he needs a haircut. "I'm Nolan."

He sits with us at the next bar. He orders oysters, and he and Lucy both slurp the slimy, half-dead things between laughs. She tells him I'm allergic to seafood because she knows I don't like to eat.

"Should I get some fries?" he asks, smiling, but I shake my head.

I have nothing to say now. I only know Lucy by secrets I can't pass under red umbrellas plastered with beer logos. The night is ruined—I am ruined. I reach for Lucy's hand under the table and squeeze, and she squeezes back. While Nolan is in the bathroom, she says, "Don't worry. We'll head back soon."

But we stay for one more round, and after, Nolan says we should come down to the house he's staying at for the summer. The backyard opens to the ocean, and "it's beautiful; you'll see."

We walk away from the lights together, Nolan leading, and Lucy and I arm in arm a few paces behind. He and Lucy sing a song I don't know. She explains that she never plays it anymore because it was from her childhood, and, in her words, "not very good," but she knows all the lyrics anyway, and they croon it into the night.

The house is dark when we reach it. "I guess my roommates are still out," Nolan says as he pushes a gate open, leading us around the house without going inside. I press close to Lucy. We've never been this far from the main drag at night. Tide sounds rupture a menacing quiet. Behind the house is a tall garden. Nolan waves us along and disappears into it. We brush past tomatoes and peppers and fat eggplants, weaving between the hoops and stakes stuck into the ground to help them grow. I've never been touched by so many tickling things. It feels like I'm walking along someone's scalp. I grip Lucy's hand until it hurts us both, but she doesn't let go until we emerge on the other side. Before us there's a little lawn, another gate, then sand and sea.

I stop just short of the water's reach. So much liquid that goes on and on. I am afraid. Nolan, already ankle-deep, turns around. "Come in! The water feels really nice."

"I can't, I'm—"

"Allergic," Lucy interrupts. "To seaweed."

"Oh man. Must be tough having so many allergies," Nolan says. Despite his sympathetic face, the way his voice echoes off the water sounds like a taunt. "Well, you don't have to come in if you don't want to. Take a seat. Enjoy the breeze." He inhales and exhales with relish. "I'm just gonna go knee-deep for a bit and come back."

Lucy turns and says quickly, "Hang out for a sec. I wanna dip my feet in a little too."

I stand clutching my elbows, sand making its way into the grooves and creases of this terrible body I wear for Lucy. It feels useless now. Lucy and Nolan become silhouettes, nearing each other, nearing a distant spot of light glancing off the ocean somewhere deep in the furrows of night.

The first time I saw Lucy, she was in the water, eyes half-lidded. She leaned toward me like I was *it*—all of it. Her naked body looks different now. More here, less there. I realize now that bodies aren't as solid as I once thought, but wobbly and changeable. Stubby nails. Overgrown hair. I can do it too.

As Lucy and Nolan come back to the shore, she gasps. Nolan stumbles in a series of chaotic splashes that give way to a sharp "What the *fuck*!"

My body is not my body anymore but a quivering mirror of Nolan. His reflection in rippling water.

"What are you doing?" Lucy runs as hard as she can toward me, her limbs dragging in the water until she finally shakes free of it and sprints across the sand.

The quivering becomes more violent, and I realize that I can't hold this shape. I have overextended myself. Nolan makes some incoherent sounds of fear and repulsion, and I know that I'm losing form. Lucy falls to her knees and tries to hold me, crying, "No no no no," and for a moment I think it's the name we gave me together, *Lo Lo Lo Lo.*

The glass bottle is in the hotel room, so Lucy tries to cup me in her small hands, cheeks glossy with tears or maybe me. I start to slip through her fingers. With no other option, she lifts her hands to her lips and swallows me in one long gulp. In her mouth I imagine her returning to our hotel room, licking the walls and sucking on the quilt, noticing for the first time since she's known me how much I rub off everywhere.

Natalya

MEDICAL EXAMINER REPORT

GROSS DESCRIPTION

The autopsy is performed approximately 26 hours after death. Permission is by the mother of the deceased. When I read your name on the toe tag, I don't believe it right away. Then I see your ankle tattoo, faded but still the same shape.

It's late, and I am alone in the morgue. I lean in close to you. I open one eye with a blue-gloved hand and stare at your dilated pupil. I press my fingers into your inflated cheeks. Through the excess tissue, I feel the familiar shape of your face in my hand.

"You can't choose the things you remember," my mother told me that afternoon while she cleaned and gutted a fish in the white mouth of my grandmother's kitchen sink. "The important things will find you."

I remember this: the sharp scent of raw fish that stuck to my mother's hands for the rest of the evening; the seaside town in rain, smelling rotten and alive at the same time; the smudges of your eyeliner as we stood under the awning of the shuttered convenience store, me with the bag of onions my mother forgot, you with the slimmest cigarette I had ever seen, like a lollipop stick between your lips.

You knew I wanted to kiss you. That's what I heard in the crackle of paper and dry tobacco each time our eyes had met in that small space. A cold wind swept in from the coast, and the coming winter cut its teeth on our ears. We didn't know each other yet. Between us there was still the strangeness of a stranger's body trapped near your own. You closed the space between us and blew smoke too close to my face. I couldn't speak, only stare at your cracked lips, plaster skin, and that round, graspable chin.

When the rain eased, you stepped back onto the sidewalk. I stayed a bit longer so I could watch you toss the cigarette butt into a puddle and walk away.

I never thought I would find you so many years later and so many miles from where we met. Yet here you are, unexpected and fruit-flesh pale. I have forgotten many things from that year. My mind smoothed out what my skin couldn't. Despite this, your dark bun and the pinkness behind your knees clings to my mind, and because of this I think you must be important.

CLINICAL SUMMARY

You, the patient, are a 41-year-old female with a medical history significant for diabetes, chronic tobacco use, COPD, and teaching me how to coax an orgasm with my tongue. For several days prior to the event that took your life, you complained of dyspnea. Your mother found you lying on the carpet in the apartment where you lived alone, only hours after your death.

Our history began in the last summer of high school. I came to your town because my grandmother died, though I never told you this. That lakeside colonial you dropped me off at was hers. My father had grown up there. He had learned to swim in that lake and spent summers cycling through those neighborhoods. Throughout my childhood, I visited my grandmother between summer camps and over long weekends, but only after her death did we spend so long in that house. It brimmed with my grandparents' long, full life. My parents didn't know what to do with its remains and had to spend a month carefully sorting, discarding. They brought me not because I was too young to be left unattended but because a few months prior, I had been sent to inpatient care for cutting myself. No one dared to leave me alone.

I saw you for the second time on a Sunday morning as I, bored and taken with its smallness, tried to swim across the tiny lake between my grandmother's house and yours. My long limbs, which had come in a sudden growth spurt the previous year, were still new to me. I thought I could catch anything within my new wing-span's breadth. Barely halfway across the water, I grew tired. I stopped to tread water, panting. I wondered if I could drown in that shallow lake. How many minutes until I stopped fighting for the surface. How many hours until my parents noticed I had not come home. How many years before people stopped thinking about me, dead or alive.

This is when you, skinny as a carving knife, emerged from the trees on the opposite bank. I recognized you immediately by the shape of your limbs and the lines your arm made as you dropped the cigarette from your mouth to your side, flicking ash. A nymph-thing masked in smoke. You looked my age, but there was something animal about the way you leaned against the tree, like you were listening. Did you see me swimming, or were you looking at something beyond my bobbing head? Was it the house, green-shuttered, green tree–flanked, or the current against our sliver of private beach?

Because I couldn't bring myself to drown in front of you, I swam back to my side of the lake. But I searched for you everywhere: the paths in the woods, the kitschy town center, the mall in the next suburb. You were nowhere until you were walking across a parking lot toward me, no longer fantastical. Just another teenager, like me.

EVIDENCE OF INJURY

Your body is entirely unscathed. No bruises, no wounds. Not so much as a bit of peeling around your fingernails. There are some new creases and stretch marks, but the texture of your skin is exactly as I remember. I always envied it.

In medical school I discovered that suicide is contagious, especially with teenagers, and this filled me with dread. I could have been the first link, dragging a chain of unknowable length into an unknowable nonexistence. I remembered you then, your mouth around the phrase, "You have to be afraid to live."

EXTERNAL EXAMINATION

You, the subject, are 62 inches tall and weigh 140 pounds. Your body is well-developed, well-nourished, albeit slightly overweight for your stated age. You have a blue-gray tattoo on your ankle: blurred Cyrillic letters. I can't read them, but I still remember how you spoke his name out loud as you sat naked before me.

There is dependent lividity, algor mortis, and rigor mortis, which keeps your arms open. I try to fold them against your sides, but they keep springing back, your tendons unwilling to release their last pose. Once, your hand flies out and almost slaps my face. My startled gasp echoes through the morgue. Before I can stop myself, I say your name aloud. I plead with you to be still. My voice sounds strange ricocheting between walls that never hold tenderness. Fluorescent bulbs buzz through the following silence like summer insects.

"You don't live here" was the first thing you said to me, a statement rather than a question. I had just unlocked my bike outside the grocery store in the town center. I couldn't identify your accent, though I could guess something Slavic in your name. When I replied that I didn't live there and I didn't know anyone, you seemed to sparkle with home-field advantage. We exchanged names. I thought the Capri Light you pulled from its pink-and-white box was a piece of candy until you lit it. You offered me one, but I declined because before we met, I had never smoked.

I was nervous for our walk, palms sweating as I dragged my bike along with us. I hardly paid attention as you pointed out places you liked among the storefronts until you stopped at the little one-screen movie theater and pointed at the marquee. "I love this place the most."

I listed moderately artistic movies I knew, hoping to impress you, even though some of them lulled me to sleep. I was reluctant to admit I had never seen your favorite, *Coffee and Cigarettes.*

You offered to watch it with me, and I caught your ash-and-soap smell for the first time as you stepped closer and said, "Come over."

I replied, "Sure," but I meant *Yes yes please yes.*

Your head is not deformed, and you have no scars. Your sclerae, cornea, and lenses are clear. Your nose and external ears are beautiful, petite, and pale like the imperfect end of a half-molten candle, but they are unremarkable, their passages clear. Your lips and gums show no lesions. Your neck is symmetrical and has no unusual masses. Your clavicle, breasts, protruding abdomen, all your flesh is unremarkable, unlike mine.

I pull up one sleeve to show you how well my scars faded even though your eyes are closed.

INTERNAL EXAMINATION (BODY CAVITIES)

On the strip of balcony outside your mother's third-floor apartment, I pretended I was having trouble with the lighter so that you would lean in close. The scrape of the wheel striking flint was crisp in our ears and contained between our cheekbones. You offered me the flame, cupped like a fluttering insect in your waxy rose lotion. I liked how your apartment faced away from the lake, toward the sea. Over your shoulder I saw the broken Maine coast, beachless and wooded, a series of lakes widening out into the Atlantic. The smoke tasted barely bitter, faint enough to keep puffing as you watched.

Inside we played the film on your computer monitor, sitting on your bed with a screw-top bottle of red blend. At first I joined you each time you opened the window and lit another Capri, dangling one arm out into the evening, but past the third I couldn't keep up.

I remember that the film was black and white and there was a lot of talking, mostly about nothing. It appears this way in my head: a few images, one or two lines of dialogue. Wrinkled faces and checkered tables, ceramic cups, and ashtrays blooming with cigarette butts. I didn't like it very much, and after a while I gave up on paying attention.

The sky blackened slowly as the sun dipped into the opposite horizon. Your room filled with cool air. There was still about a quarter left in the movie when you tossed your shirt aside and unclasped your bra. The rest of the evening is a blur of fingers and teeth. On the brink of your second orgasm, I realized the film was ending because it was silent and completely dark, your breath caught in that hitch of anticipation before you came.

As you smoked again afterward, limbs dribbling into the moon-wet night, I noticed the lettering on your ankle. When I asked what it was, you turned from the misty window. Your tongue flicked Artur's name in a way mine never could. The love of your life, an older man from your hometown. I grew anxious as you told the story and began to gather my clothing quickly. I had never been on any side of unfaithfulness. I felt naive when you laughed and said, "Don't worry, he lets me fool around."

I wonder what happened with Artur. All I know about your relationship is that photo you showed me decades ago, the two of you on a rooftop in Moscow, a place you promised you'd return to. Your file cites you as a US citizen with an address in this city, unmarried. As I make the first incision, your hand finds my waist. Your fingers brush my hip like you're reaching for me. I hold your arm down with my elbow and push the blade deeper.

The standard thoracic incisions are made. Your pleural cavities contain a moderate amount of clear yellow fluid that I must measure, reduce what's inside you to cc's. I unravel you on the cold table. I split a seam through your center, tug and rearrange the jeweled yellow fat. Everything within is slick, threatening to slip from my grasp. I catalog every centimeter of you, weigh each organ with equal care. Your skeletal muscles are dark red-brown, of normal firmness and bulk. Your rib cage is intact. There are many things I never asked you. Even with my hands around your heart, my fingers tracing your vertebrae, you are a stranger.

HEART: I first saw my wife from afar too. On a blinding January afternoon, I passed her sitting alone in a classroom, on the way to my advisor's office. The tight, tumbling chaos of her hair writhed in the sunlight. She flipped a page in her book and didn't look up to notice how long I watched her before I walked along. I never told anyone this story until now—how mythical she looked then with dark eyelashes, thick eyebrows, a round face like a thumbprint in her curls. We met later in the same study-abroad group. She introduced herself as Emma, and though I had never heard her name, my heart rioted in my chest, *I know I know I know I know you.*

Emma doesn't know about you. I never thought she would need to. I recount all this because it was nothing like when you told me your name in front of the grocery store. My whole being stilled at the sound of your voice—muscles, organs, mind. Rigor mortis. You finally understand how it feels.

With its fat peeled off, your heart weighs 296 grams, heavier than average. The walls are thickened by calcified yellow plaques. The myocardium, in contrast, is soft and mottled. I describe you with words I've written countless times. Smooth. Moderate. Transparent. Yet you were never any of these things.

GENITOURINARY SYSTEM: After we started hanging out, I told my parents I'd befriended a few local kids, and they were happy to drop me off wherever to meet up with them. Really it was just you, but they didn't ask questions. They were relieved to have me out of the house, where they listened to my every step and tensed whenever they heard silence.

My mother and I kept a strict routine when I returned home each evening. I stripped down to my underwear, and she checked every inch of me for fresh cuts. When she was done, we spent the rest of the night in front of the television. My father joined us to watch a late-night talk show. They asked about my day, but each question felt heavy with the big unanswerable ones they never voiced. My father placed one hand on my shoulder and left it there for a long time. My mother watched me the way she must have watched my mouth open and close when I first lay beside her. Each act of affection was a small humiliation.

Your right kidney weighs 111 grams, and the left weighs 120. Your bladder and uterus are normal. You have never carried a child.

GASTROINTESTINAL SYSTEM: Most afternoons I spent with you seem indistinguishable now—hotboxing your mother's SUV, driving aimlessly while the trees sipped and swallowed the sun. I saw every shade of your face on those roads, the painted yellow and white lines ticking past your sunglasses. While my parents emptied my grandmother's house, stripped all the places touched by our family's fingertips, I cataloged your features, white and gold and pink and blue, then flickering in and out of the dark with each passing streetlight.

In sparse towns we found quiet streets to park and fold down the rear seats. The nearest houses glimmered faintly between the trees. The windows fogged up from our bodies, sticky and panting in the air-conditioning. On clear days the crickets were deafening, and on others we listened to the rain. Curled up with me in the back of your mother's car in pitch-black, you traced your fingers over the ridges on my thigh.

"I knew a girl in Moscow who did this kind of thing," you whispered one evening, tapping the marred tissue. *Click, hiss*; your cheek and lips came up in quivering snatches of yellow and gold, then disappeared. "I don't get it. Why?"

I could have told you about each scar then. How the first cut was an accident. While helping with dinner, I was careless with my mother's sharpest kitchen knife. I didn't recall how it slipped, only that when the crisp mark swelled with blood, my heart suddenly returned to my chest: *I know I know I know.*

"It feels good," I said, unable to explain anything more. I followed the cherry in an arc to the gap in the back window. I imagined Artur lying like this by your knee in the cinder-block apartment complex where you met. My nostrils filled with smoke.

You switched on the car light and climbed to the front seat, skin sallow under the tiny bulb. The glove box fell open with a *thunk*. You returned with your mother's Swiss Army knife, and I held my breath as you sat cross-legged and slit the inside of your leg. A tiny red streak appeared, bubbling until a thin line slid down your thigh. I had an impulse to lick it up, tease the opening with my tongue.

"It stings," you said.

I pressed one finger next to the wound to find that it barely cracked. "You didn't go deep enough."

You lay down and rested your head on my leg. "I'm afraid of blood. I can't look at it any longer. It makes me sick."

I wasn't sure if it was the blood that made you sick or if it was me. My skin gave away how many times I had done this, how much more blood I'd drawn. "You didn't have to do that," I said.

If you had asked, I might have explained how I stole one of the X-ACTO knives from the art studio at school and tucked it under my mattress. I started out very careful. I enjoyed the power of counting secret wounds for several months, though the nights I made them were murky. My game ended one evening when my mother returned home from work early. I stood before her in my towel, damp and exposed, and she looked me up and down with her house keys still clutched in one hand. She slapped me and began to cry.

Instead you asked, "What are you afraid of?"

I thought of the lake. The green water turned my scars into ripples and my limbs into disappearing things, unrecognizable. "Nothing," I said.

You laughed. "That's stupid."

"Why?" I took a napkin from the center console and wiped up your blood.

"You have to be afraid to live."

You sat up. I realized it was almost ten, and you called Artur at eleven each day. We dressed, and you drove me home, the Swiss Army knife rattling in the glove box each time you turned.

Your gallbladder is surgically absent, a no-show to our reunion. All the parts of you that could have once been sick are what we call grossly normal and unremarkable, no tumors or ulcers to be found. I check your thigh for that cut, but it was so shallow it didn't leave a mark.

ENDOCRINE SYSTEM: I can't examine your thyroid because of the limitations of this autopsy, so I will just write this: when I'm asked why, I remember being fourteen at a fitness class in school when I saw myself in the mirror, working the candy-bright dumbbells up and down, my sneakers squeaking off the hardwood, thudding onto the plastic step, and staring right into my sweat-polished face, I thought, *what am I doing here*, and then, *what am I*, and suddenly the clapperboard hit my throat, and my blood screamed, *cut, cut, cut*, and the whole scene was reduced to a tick-marked screen behind a long, fat lens, and I squinted, trying to make out where the set ended or what lay beyond it but I couldn't, the lights were too bright and I didn't know who I was outside the script and the dumbbells slipped from my grip and hit the ground and there is still a dent on that floor and I haven't been able to forget my own eyes since.

RETICULOENDOTHELIAL SYSTEM: Your spleen has substance, is slightly enlarged and firm, which I find ironic. I never moved or upset you. I never even heard you raise your voice.

The first time Emma saw me naked, she stopped everything to stare. She ran her hands along the marks just like you did once. "If I ever see a fresh one, this is over," she said with a hard edge to her voice, and I nodded, assuring her, "I'm past it." Like this, we lied into each other's mouths for the rest of our lives.

The temptation never left me. I'm in my best years now. I see a therapist once a week, and nothing bad happens if I skip a session. Still, sometimes I think about every kitchen knife we have, black handles jutting out of their wooden block.

Emma, with her fierce heels and unflinching cerise mouth, never has patience for finicky painters and catty art dealers. Despite this, she gives me chance after chance because we all have to be weak to something.

An incision in your spleen reveals a small imperfection: an area of infarction, pale as a pink moon.

LUNGS: The rest of that summer passed in a swift daze. My parents cleared out my grandmother's house. Rugs rolled up; furniture and antiques sold; the books, clothing, and kitchenware picked off from the lawn during several tag sales. Everything else in a bin at the nearest Goodwill. We filled a rented van with the important things: photo albums, family heirlooms, my grandfather's glasses. Soon the house was empty.

I can no longer pinpoint the last evening you and I spent together, but I remember taking one final dip in the lake before we drove home. The water in Maine is never warm, even at the end of summer. I stared up at the stretch of flat blue, strands of clouds like scar tissue across it, and wondered if I should tell you I was leaving, whether you would care. I tried to imagine what you would say, but I could only picture you sitting cross-legged on the balcony, shrugging, taking a drag, and not looking at me. Staring out at the sea that separated you from someone else. Fear, colder than lake water, slithered into my veins. My body came alive at something so petty. I pulled my head underwater. Bubbles flew from my mouth and nose, but I couldn't ignore the ache in my chest as the last of my breath left me. I surfaced into the creamy sky coughing.

I received your text the week later: *Hey, are you around?* I wasn't, so I didn't reply, and you never contacted me again.

Your lungs have a combined weight of 723 grams. They are the usual shape but full of carbon and plaques. You must have switched from Capri Lights to something harsh and heavy even though you had told me that thick, stubby cigarettes looked ugly in a woman's fingers. I imagine you felt death come for you. I picture you lighting a cigarette on some balcony in the city, waiting. Instead of traffic, you heard pines chatter in the wind and tides lap the soil.

I'm sorry I never said goodbye.

EXTREMITIES: I pull back your skin, looking for everything I never understood about you. I put my fingers in your mouth, feel around your teeth. Your tongue is dry. You don't even twitch when I prod your uvula. Your nipples, soft and wide, won't bead up if I pinch them. If I pluck your rib cage, you won't recoil. No matter how I touch you, you remain still, peeled apart like a pithy citrus.

I seal the fissures and wipe the smears from your skin. I try to arrange your body symmetrically, but your limbs and breasts keep falling askew. There is so much more to you—stomach folds and dimpled thighs. The girl from that summer was only a sliver of the person you would become. I lean in and hold your round face in both my hands, your earlobe's familiar fit in the crook between my thumb and forefinger. Obscenely, I still want to kiss you. I want to bite your cheek to see if it tastes the same. Instead I release you and pull the sheet over your face. This is the last time I see you.

CLINICOPATHOLOGIC CORRELATION

Emma and I spent a semester in Italy. We spoke the language better than our classmates, so while they were in Rome and Florence, we stayed alone in a small town with a university that only offered classes in Italian. We often had coffee before class, dinner on pleasant evenings. My host family had a beautiful garden and patio where we would sit with wine, a soda-can ashtray, and a Marlboro between my fingertips, talking for hours after everyone had gone to sleep. One hot night, our faces barely lit by the splatter of yellow windows and sickle moon, I kissed her.

"I was wondering how long it would take," she said as I pulled back. I thought of you then, how you cornered me between the movie and your window. You never waited.

You died naturally of acute myocardial infarction. After I shut you away in a drawer, I wonder if I was trying to recreate my evenings with you that first summer with Emma. Hold a mirror to the last time I wanted to devour someone cheek first.

SUMMARY AND REFLECTION

I don't know if I loved you, yet you linger within me like an apparition. I carved my deepest cut right before I took the MCAT. I still have a slanted seam across my forearm. It needed many stitches, and the doctors told me I was lucky my hand remained steady after it healed. That night, with the shower running, the tiles turning red all around me, I thought of the tiny slit on your leg and how much that hair-thin wound hurt you. As I fainted, the sound of water became the engine of your mother's SUV, the rush of the highway, and then your breath in my ear.

Persimmons

The persimmon tree in the courtyard had always called to Uma. Some nights she dreamt it was full of fat, enticing fruit while the land around it lay stark. The settlers had found their colony just like that, empty except for this thriving tree, but Uma had never seen the sorry plant bear anything. Her mother's garden flourished around the dead persimmon tree until the morning Uma woke up to find it impossibly green.

"Mother," Uma said, entering the kitchen in her robe.

"I know," her mother replied from the stove. She had been awake for some time already. A cup of hot milk tea steamed on Uma's side of the table, and breakfast was underway. Uma sat and cupped the mug to warm her hands. New leaves shuddered beyond the sliding doors facing the garden. The tree had been bare for hundreds of years. Not a single bud had emerged in Uma's mother's life, nor her grandmother's, nor her great-grandmother's. Everyone expected it to be the same for Uma's, and yet.

"We've got a busy day ahead," Uma's mother said from the kitchen, as though it was a weeding day and not the end of everything. She was a cold woman with beautiful hands. The most comfort she ever offered Uma was two fingers rubbing menthol ointment on her chest when she was sick. They hardly touched otherwise and tried their best not to ask each other for much. Still, Uma loved those hands, loved to hear them work—the spatula sliding between pan and popping egg, a paring knife scraping through not-quite-ripe fruit.

Uma's mother set down their breakfast plates. Only hers had golden plum slices. Uma tried to reach for one, but her mother yanked her plate closer, away from Uma's fingers.

"What does it matter now?" Uma asked, slashing open her egg yolk.

"It matters most now."

Uma's mother picked up a slice and bit. Uma closed her eyes to hear it crunch between her mother's teeth. Over the years Uma had learned to tell ripeness from sound alone and had imagined the taste from what she'd read and heard. The pause between pressure and give was too long, the scrape too crisp. It was sour. Her mother chewed it down anyway, spiteful even on Uma's last morning.

Uma knew her fate already. Their planet, a small one on the far reaches of human colonization, was tied to her lineage. Of all the explorers who had come down to observe the single flourishing plant on a barren globe, the tree chose one. It spoke to her as she slept in the vessel orbiting its gravitational pull. It lured her with the promise of fertility. When she accepted, a valley of beautiful, arable land appeared on the planet, and a child formed in her womb. The tree remained bare since and only asked two things: that nobody with her blood should eat the fruit borne from their promise, and that she let the tree have one of her children when it was hungry.

The children learned this in school during a history lecture that drew all eyes in the classroom to Uma. She had spent her life moving between these moments of self-awareness, forgetting what she was, and then remembering suddenly, violently. The teacher pulled up slides of grotesque artwork detailing what might—but very likely wouldn't, they said—happen to Uma. She hugged her arms on top of her desk, pressed her fingers deep into her own arm flesh just to be sure it was still in one piece. Her classmates took in illustration after illustration of the tree tearing women apart and avoided Uma from then on, as if prophecy could be contagious.

Uma always thought fate was a choice. She believed that like her mother, Uma would be free the moment she had a daughter to carry the tree's burden. Once she finished school, Uma picked a boy and began to track her temperature each day. She poked holes in a pack of condoms with a fine sewing needle. But that morning she learned that fate had her in its grasp from the moment she squirmed into the world, before anything could grow in her own womb.

Uma was raised in a house of many empty rooms. The wooden structure encircled a garden that had been in their family for generations, the old tree at its center. Two porches wrapped around the house's entirety, one facing the courtyard and the other along the outer walls. Only she and her mother lived in it since her grandmother had died over a decade ago. All but a few rooms were full of shadowy, sheeted furniture. Hidden creatures beyond half-open doors, they had frightened Uma since she was young. On hot summer days she lay in cool, undisturbed hallways and whispered to the furniture's amorphous shapes, asking them to spare her.

"Why don't we move out?" Uma asked her mother in the garden one afternoon. "This house is too big for us."

Her mother dropped her spade and grabbed Uma by the shoulder, turning her toward the withered tree they would never cut down. "Make no mistake," her mother said. "Every voice in your head is that tree. You couldn't leave it if you tried."

One room had always been padlocked and off-limits. Uma had asked and asked and tried to look through her mother's things once or twice for the key, but had never entered. After breakfast, her mother handed her a heavy gold key. Uma didn't have to ask which lock it fit.

The door opened easily for something shut so long. The small wooden chamber had nothing but a book at its center and carvings scrawled on the far wall. They showed the naked tree dotted with fruit, just like in Uma's dreams. She pressed her fingers into the tree trunk and the pieces of girl etched into it. Uma thought again of the paintings from history class. Her mother must have seen the same slides in the same classroom decades before her and also imagined herself rent limb from limb, but Uma's mother never shared these things. Uma wondered how her mother had been treated between that lesson and Uma's birth, and whether those unmentioned years were the reason why she lived in such shame, avoiding any mention of their birthright. She was herself a closed door, a padlock, a key that Uma felt certain she would die without finding.

Uma picked up the old book bound with twine. Within she found all those same paintings. Only then did it occur to her that she had never seen them in person, not at a local history museum, nor at their small library or town meeting hall. She never questioned why, eager to wipe them from her thoughts as soon as class let out. Past the paintings were pages of instructions in handwriting hauntingly like her own, as though she'd written her own fate.

She brought the book to the kitchen, but her mother wasn't there. The dishes sat unwashed in the sink. The garden was empty too. At last Uma spotted her mother's straight back across the courtyard, her tanned neck catching the morning light. She spread her arms wide as she threw open the doors to all their disused rooms. In sweeping motions, she pulled the sheets from the furniture. Long tables and countless dining chairs emerged. Cushioned seating and low stools. Paintings, sculptures. Large and lavish entertainment spaces bloomed from the recesses of their home. Twirling from one piece to another, kicking discarded sheets out of her path, her mother looked like a dancer. Uma could watch her move all day.

Truthfully, Uma never cultivated any dreams beyond the notion of leaving. She had some vague sense of wanting to see other worlds.

She read books about pirates and explorers like the ones who had settled their planet, and imagined she could be one of them. She never understood why her mother seemed content to tend their flower garden for the birthdays, anniversaries, and funerals in their valley. It was such a small existence.

Uma felt it most keenly when their valley hit summer and deep-space tourists descended into their atmosphere. Their garden was busiest then. Travelers loved to marvel at the dead tree and hear the planet's history straight from Uma's mother. Some teenagers from town collected admission while Uma worked the flower stand. The first year Uma was allowed to work the tour season, her mother made her swear she would never act like this was her home, never act like they were related in front of customers. Uma accepted these terms readily in return for an allowance. She and her mother rarely went anywhere together to begin with, so it wasn't hard to pretend to be strangers. The townspeople played along, and Uma eventually understood that she, rather than the tree, was their prized possession, what the tourists wanted to get their hands on most.

"Our planet is really strange," Uma said as they closed shop at the end of one of these long summer days, turning away stragglers who had missed the final admission.

"Yes," Uma's mother said, latching the front gate. "So are we."

"What are other planets like?"

Her mother shrugged. "I don't know."

"Can we take a trip?"

Her mother scoffed but didn't answer, disappearing into the kitchen.

It was difficult for Uma to picture life outside their valley, although she studied what she could. Because they were so far from their planet of origin, most media never reached them uncorrupted, and new technologies rarely survived the long journey. They had reference books and fiction, but an actual life was some vague thing in between. Or maybe this was just the tree turning everything murky inside Uma's mind.

Uma biked into the farmland surrounding their town. They needed manure, fresh milk, and a handful of other supplies. She loved early summer mornings. The sky was clearest in those weeks between thaw and heat, and she could see every treetop on the lush mountains that ringed their valley. Vehicles slowed as she pedaled by, their occupants staring, scrutinizing her body for some evidence of what they knew would come. She kept her head high and gazed ahead until the barn on the horizon loomed tall. A familiar face waited on the wide drive leading up to it. The boy she had chosen. Uma waved, and he walked toward her.

"Moon," she said, unsure of how else to greet him. *Good morning* seemed inappropriate. *Hello* felt strange.

Moon gripped her handlebars. "How are you holding up?"

"You heard, then."

"The whole town has heard by now." He picked the notebook out from wagon tailing her bike. "Leave your bike here; I'll drive us back. My parents sent me to help with preparations."

Uma released her bike reluctantly. She wished she'd known that bike ride would be her last. She might have gone slower, savored it.

They entered the barn, where they had spent their adolescence getting high and sticking fingers and tongues wherever they wanted. Uma chose Moon because things were always fun with him. She felt most human pinned down under his weight, laughter tumbling out of her like she was any other girl. Her mind, which was already beginning to feel distant from her body, was more settled now that she was with him.

That day the barn was restless. Frenzied cows moaned deafeningly. Moon knelt down, tilting his head sideways to look under the gates. The ground was sticky with milk, seeping freely from each pained animal's nipples. "It's really happening, then," he whispered.

"Moon." Uma knelt beside him and leaned her head on his shoulder. "Let's leave."

Moon's truck caught the sun and pulled it down the road with them toward the mountains. Wide swaths of farmland separated the barn from the tree line. They sped past prying eyes of farmhands and livestock, driving fast because they were running from everything. Uma remembered when Moon had gotten this truck, a gift for his sixteenth birthday. It came with the stipulation, of course, that he would need to help around the farm more, and he did. Moon was good in many ways. She wasn't the only girl to undress in his truck bed, but she was the only one who would never say anything sweet to him. He didn't ask where they were going. He never really asked her questions. He knew who she was—everyone did—but she could almost see the shutters close behind his eyes when they were together. He didn't want to think about her fate even when it was imminent, but she couldn't tell if this was out of affection or indifference or fear.

Uma had never understood love, maybe because she was never meant to give or receive it—not from her mother, not from anyone. But with her hand on Moon's knee, her bare feet resting on his truck's dashboard, she wanted badly to leave something behind. Maybe that stickiness was a kind of love. Even if she was gone everywhere else, she hoped some trace of her would linger in his passenger seat, the whole sweat-flower-fertilizer suite of her smell.

The trees swallowed them suddenly. The road narrowed, a shallow canopy blocking the sky. Light came through muffled and trembling. Uma grabbed Moon's arm as they reached a trailhead. "Do you think it goes all the way to the top?"

"I don't know," he replied, braking. "I've never hiked it."

They left Moon's truck parked on the road and started up the trail. The forest turned quickly dense. Light became indistinguishable from color. The moss coating every stone and tree trunk glowed in jewel tones. Moon's skin took on a deeper hue under the bottle-glass cast of foliage. The old woods held a heavy, moist quiet, like an animal's breath. After a short while, the incline grew steeper, and the path nearly disappeared. Uma pushed onward, stepping over roots and hoisting herself over boulders, but Moon stopped. "Is this a good idea?"

"Good or bad doesn't matter anymore." Uma looked down at Moon. He seemed small and young, leaning on a tree trunk to catch his breath. It was like they were children again, chasing each other through haystacks as Uma's mother bought supplies at the farm stand. Uma had always outrun him. "As long as we keep going up, the trees will thin."

"But how far is that?"

"I don't care."

"Uma." Moon walked to the boulder Uma stood on and touched her calf gently. "You know there's nothing there."

Of course she knew. They'd all seen the aerial photos of their planet, a splotch of green and gold and blue stamped into gray, but it was no longer enough for her. Uma wanted to see that vast nothingness herself, stretching to a black horizon. See the air they breathe thin into a halo of color before it dissipated.

"You can go back if you want." Uma turned and continued. After a pause, Moon followed.

A clearing appeared not far ahead, a bright gash between the trees. Uma eagerly picked up her pace. Moon caught up just as they stumbled out into a grassy clearing. Above, sky. To their left, the road to Moon's farm.

"I don't understand," Moon said. "We were going up. We went up."

"That fucking tree." Uma lay in the grass, still sweaty from what she thought was a climb. Though the journey had felt hours long, the sun had barely budged. Uma thought of all her mother's silences. She must have tried too. What could she have said?

Moon bent down and offered his hand to help Uma up like they were in gym class, recovering from a sprint. His warm, square-jawed face, the white slash of sunlight in his sleek hair. Uma almost cried. She wanted to rip his arms off. She wanted to bury her face in his grassy smell. She took his hand. "Let's find your truck."

By the time they returned to Uma's house, preparations were underway. The conservatory had booked their best musicians for the banquet. Every bakery and restaurant had sent platters of food; the brewery had sent barrel after barrel. The paper mill had provided crates of handmade lanterns that looked like ripe persimmons. The bell rang so often that eventually Uma's mother left the door unlocked. Packages accumulated in the front hallway, crammed beside rain boots and shoes. Uma realized quickly that this would be a night of celebration, not mourning.

Moon seemed a little sorry at least. "Why does it have to be such a spectacle?" he asked from a step stool, arms outstretched.

Uma handed him a lantern. "It's rare."

He hammered it to the awning of the courtyard-facing porch. When he finished, he sat on the stool, gazing over Uma's shoulder at the tree. Without looking, she felt it stir. The flowers had already opened and begun to take on color. "It's not pretty," Moon said quietly, as though the tree might hear.

"Spectacles aren't always pretty." She passed Moon another lantern. She knew he wanted to say more, but she was afraid— she didn't want to know if his feelings would make her feel sad or feel nothing. Her mother called from inside just then, saving them from the embarrassment of attempting tenderness after so many years.

"It should fit you perfectly," Uma's mother said as she and Uma stood over the ceremonial garment made of waxy green foliage from the tree's first flowering.

"How is it still fresh?" Uma asked, leaning in close. The whole dress smelled like a just-snipped stem.

Her mother sat on the bed and stroked one leaf with her fingertip. "It wasn't until today." She had hardly looked at her daughter all day. Uma thought about stroking her mother's shoulder the same way, with one finger. She wondered if her mother's skin would feel like the leaves.

"I tried to leave," Uma admitted. "This morning."

Her mother shook her head. "You should have known better."

"I had to try. You never let me."

That same scoff. "Why do you think that is?"

"Will you have another daughter after me?"

Uma's mother nodded slowly. "I have to."

Uma pictured a girl who was rocked and held. Her mother making flower crowns and smiling. "Can't you act like you want to be my mother, just for today?" Uma asked softly. She wanted to feel like something that could be loved, if only for one night.

"No," her mother replied, never one to sugarcoat. "I'm sorry. I can't."

That night the townspeople gathered in high spirits to eat and drink alongside Uma. Her fear dissipated in a fog of alcohol and festivity. She felt more carefree than she had imagined she would on the nights she lay awake, thinking about this evening. With the end in sight, Uma didn't have to behave. She kicked off her shoes and ate with her hands, drank straight from the bottle. She danced with everyone, kissed anyone. She treated it like a liberation.

Drunk and bitter, Uma crossed the courtyard through the flowers to where her mother sat inside the house, beside a table covered in fruit. Uma collapsed over a massive bowl of late-season peaches, resting her cheek on their velvety flesh. "Which one did you eat first?" she asked, picking up a pear slice from a nearby platter and holding it to her mother's throat like a knife.

Her mother pried the slice out of Uma's fingers. "I started small," her mother said. "With a grape."

Uma knew the story well. Her grandmother had placated Uma with it when she was a child and still whined about wanting to eat fruit, mostly because it was something she wasn't allowed to have. Her mother got pregnant while she was a teenager, eager to be rid of her curse. She woke from a long, difficult labor and demanded every fruit Uma's grandmother could get her hands on. Uma's mother ate a bite of everything before she held Uma for the first time, taking the child in her arms only when she screamed for milk. Her grandmother promised Uma that her mother would do the same for her when she had a daughter.

"How did it taste?" Uma asked, bringing her face close to her mother's. Their features were nearly identical, but her mother's seemed more elegant. It was as though the only thing Uma had inherited from her unknown father was a lack of grace.

"Delicious," her mother replied cruelly. Uma slapped her. It was easy for them to be terrible to each other. People started to watch. The sting of her mother's skin on Uma's palm felt good, so she pulled her hand back to hit her again, but Moon grabbed her arm and yanked her away.

"Don't do this," he said.

Uma shrugged him off and snatched up the bowl before her. She rolled all but one peach onto the table and filled the bowl with one of every variety of fruit in the spread. The room around them went quiet. A few whispers broke through, no doubt debating whether someone should stop her. Uma grabbed Moon's hand and pushed into the hallway, and the crowd let her go only because they saw how he could temper her.

The house brimmed with bodies. Everyone they passed pressed close, wanting to touch Uma. They were red-faced, sticky-fingered. People she saw every day sickened her. Her fourth-grade teacher grabbed some of her hair and smelled it. The woman who owned the bakery wiped up the sweat on the back of Uma's neck and licked it from her hand.

"This way." Moon changed directions and tugged Uma into the foyer and out the front door. The night air was cooler there than in the courtyard. The mountains cut off the sky in a jagged black line. Uma realized this would be the last time she set foot beyond the courtyard.

"Do you think you'll ever leave this place?"

Moon, already a few paces ahead, stopped to look back at her. "I don't know. The farm, you know. Someone has to take it over."

She sighed. "You're so lame. Hike the mountains at least."

He squinted at the horizon. "We tried. Is it even possible?"

"It will be if I'm not with you."

Moon helped Uma crawl through her bedroom window as he had on many nights. She had a corner room with windows facing both directions. Moon closed the courtyard curtains, and Uma turned to shut the outside window. She paused to look at the stars. A patch of grass trembled, and she leaned forward, hoping to catch a small animal, but nothing emerged, and eventually it became still again.

Moon undressed Uma like he was peeling her open. She could tell he loved her, but only when he pretended she was just a girl. He never wanted to really see her, and he had no interest in saving her. Uma belonged to no one, not even herself.

Straddling Moon, she fed him each fruit from the bowl. "Tell me how it tastes," she demanded between gasps, and he gave barely coherent replies about tart and juicy and grainy—things she knew just from hearing his teeth cut into the fruit flesh. All night she pressed sweet things into his mouth, even when it was full and dripping, even when he shook his head or coughed. Empathy and conscience ebbed out of her with each slick piece she shoved between his teeth. When the tree tore her apart, she hoped something inside Moon would tear too.

Uma met the morning alone and naked. It was barely light out. The lanterns still burned in the courtyard, casting a red glow over the inner window. "Did you have any?" her mother's silhouette asked from the doorway, pointing to the half-eaten fruit strewn across the bed.

Uma sat up. "No, just Moon."

"The bath is ready." Her mother stepped out of sight, leaving the door open.

Uma walked through the hallway in the same robe she wore to breakfast every morning, the one her mother gave her last year on the day Uma turned eighteen. Through the windows she had a clear view of the courtyard, packed with townspeople sitting in the flowers, waiting. Some turned to watch her, eyes hungry. The tree beyond blazed orange, nearly ready to bear fruit.

The ceremonial washroom—unused until now, like many of the house's other rooms—had nothing but a large, wooden tub filled with warm milk and fallen leaves. The air was humid and smelled of cream and honey. Uma stepped into the mixture of milk from every mother in town, animal and human. Viscous liquid coated her skin.

A stool scraped across the room. Her mother's butter and fresh-cut flower scent drew near.

Uma's mother ladled milk with a wide wooden bowl and poured it over her daughter's exposed neck and shoulders, then massaged it gently into her hair. "The first bath only had human milk. Just enough to fill this bowl," she said. "Do they still tell you that in school?"

Uma nodded. "Hardly a bath." The tree's calls grew stronger, a staticky fizz in her skull that made her mother sound like a stranger.

"When I was pregnant, I had terrible nightmares. Bloody, vicious. I can't even describe them now. I knew something would happen once you were born."

Uma hummed. She wasn't sure whether she heard her mother's voice or trickling milk or the leaves breaking off their branches one by one. Her mother, sensing Uma slipping, dropped the bowl and held Uma's face in both hands, tilting it to meet her gaze. "Are you listening? Have you ever heard me?" Uma blinked at her like she was looking into a warped mirror. "I wanted to be your mother, I really did," her mother continued. "But how could I? You were never mine. You came out of me the color of a ripe persimmon, eyes wide, and not a single sound coming from you. It was terrifying how inhuman you looked. You hardly saw me, and you reached at the window for that tree like it could hold you. Even now. Look at me. Me. I'm your mother."

Uma wondered if humanity was something she had been born with or something she had tried and failed to cultivate. It was clear to her now that the town never saw her or her mother as anything close to human. Was it something the tree took or never gave? Uma vaguely recognized the shape of her mother's hands against her cheeks—long, slim, cut by fine lines. "They're beautiful," she said. She'd never told her mother this.

Her mother's eyebrows drew in. Her expression was oddly glossy, like she might cry. Uma had never seen her cry. "No. Fuck them," her mother said finally. Uma only nodded.

Alone in all that souring milk, Uma's guts quickly ripened, growing softer with each moment. She felt high and hazy. She closed her eyes and tried to picture every beautiful thing she had known. The valley, the flowers, her mother's wrists. A fresh sheet of notebook paper against the wood grain of her school desk. The texture of Moon's tongue. The whir of her bike spokes as she coasted down the slight slope between the town center and her house. Fresh bread. The garden after rain, each leaf like a polished stone. Maybe there would be a trace of her left in all of it: the wet, pungent earth; the sun smell of every summer afternoon.

Uma walked back to her room still dripping. A thousand beady eyes peered at her from the twilit courtyard. She pulled on the ceremonial garment, the leaves clinging to her like a second skin. She felt naked and light, ready. She would be a martyr. The townspeople would paint her for centuries, write poems about her newborn-baby smell, how beautifully she had come apart.

Persimmons

As the sun pinked Uma's curtained window, she couldn't stop thinking about it—things coming apart. How satisfying it was to wrench weeds out with her bare hands. Crush a perfect flower in her palm. Rip Moon's skin with her teeth. Scream as she flung herself off the dock, limbs flying out until the cold lake smacked her hard. Tear, break, crumple. The ecstasy of ruin.

She remembered her mother's face, all the hatred in her pretty lips and black eyebrows. Uma took a peeled orange from her sheets and sank her teeth straight into the pith. Her mouth filled with sharp, tart liquid. Her tongue found sweetness. She drank, vampiric, sucking out the juice, smearing it on her face with both hands, gasping between drags. She crammed the remaining skin into her mouth and swallowed it, almost choking. She ate all the seeds. When she finished, she wiped her face with the milky towel and threw back the curtains, entering the courtyard through the open window.

———

The crowd parted for Uma as soon as her feet touched the ground. Nobody dared to come near her. The tree's branches swayed horribly as she approached, as though caught in a tempest. When she reached the trunk, the thickest roots writhed underground, and the town fell to its knees. Branches reached for her and she opened her arms to be pierced all over, her softened flesh giving easily to their blunt ends. The tree shed all its leaves in one ecstatic shudder that wrenched Uma apart in a single, swift motion. It chewed her bones and made pulp from her skin. Once her body was gone, she could see the town clearly, watching rapt from a bed of leaves. Fruit pushed ripe from her many arms. The heavy red globes fell upon the townspeople, who scrambled for them. Juice ran from their mouths. Her mother stared up from the front of the crowd, smiling. She saw the unnatural fruit flesh and knew. Beyond the courtyard and over the town's roof tiles, a wind swept in from between the mountains. The valley withered. The townspeople continued to eat even when all the fruit was gone. They bit down on any soft flesh they found, tearing, crunching. The crowd swallowed her mother. Her mother swallowed the crowd. The courtyard became one large mouth, and Uma twirled at its center, arms outstretched.

Acknowledgments

Thank you to:

Rachel Kim, Rola Harb, Angeline Rodriguez, and the team at Astra House for helping me bring this collection into the world.

The readers and editors of *CRAFT Literary*, *One Story*, and *Cutleaf* for giving these stories their first homes.

Manuel Gonzalez, Stuart Nadler, Derek Palacio, Dariel Suarez, Justin Torres, and Claire Vaye Watkins for guidance.

Alex Gaertner, Caro Claire Burke, Ariel Martinez, Kaycie Hall, Davin Malasarn, Anna Gazmarian, Zachary Spence, Raymond Bellinger, and my Tin House workshop for community.

Samantha Scott for patiently answering late-night texts about autopsies and wolf C-sections.

All the friends and acquaintances whose names and little facts I borrowed.

Mary J. for pushing me through the uncertainty.

Melissa Lozada-Oliva and William Zhang for talking about everything.

Ma and Baba for support, Jishnu for sanity.

Priya for knowing.

& Andrew for your love, always.

About the Author

Puloma Ghosh is a fiction writer based in Chicago whose work has appeared in *One Story, CRAFT Literary,* and *Cutleaf.* This is her first book.

The team at Astra House would like to thank
everyone who helped to publish *Mouth*.

PUBLISHER
Ben Schrank

EDITORIAL
Rola Harb

CONTRACTS
Stella Iselin

PUBLICITY
Rachael Small
Alexis Nowicki

MARKETING
Tiffany Gonzalez
Sarah Christensen Fu

SALES
Jack W. Perry

DESIGN
Jacket: Rodrigo Corral Studio
Frances DiGiovanni
Interior: Alissa Theodor

PRODUCTION
Lisa Taylor

MANAGING EDITORIAL
Olivia Dontsov

COPYEDITING
Kaitlyn San Miguel
John Vasile

COMPOSITION
Westchester Publishing Services